LOSING THE MOON

TETON MOUNTAIN SERIES
BOOK 5

KELLIE COATES GILBERT

Copyright © 2025 by Kellie Coates Gilbert

All rights reserved.

No part of this book may be reproduced in any form or by any electronic or mechanical means, including information storage and retrieval systems, without written permission from the author, except for the use of brief quotations in a book review.

Cover design: Kim Killion /The Killion Group

*For Luke Cunningham, aka Moldy Cheese
My nephew is in the health fight of his life.
He's my hero.*

PRAISE FOR THE NOVELS OF KELLIE COATES GILBERT:

"If you're looking for a new author to read, you can't go wrong with Kellie Coates Gilbert."
~**Lisa Wingate**, NY Times bestselling author of *Before We Were Yours*

"Well-drawn, sympathetic characters and graceful language"
~**Library Journal**

"Deft, crisp storytelling"
~**RT Book Reviews**

"I devoured the book in one sitting."
~**Chick Lit Central**

"Gilbert's heartfelt fiction is always a pleasure to read."
~**Buzzing About Books**

"Kellie Coates Gilbert delivers emotionally gripping plots and authentic characters."

~**Life Is Story**

"I laughed, I cried, I wanted to throw my book against the wall, but I couldn't quit reading."
~**Amazon reader**

"I have read other books I had a hard time putting down, but this story totally captivated me."
~**Goodreads reader**

"I became somewhat depressed when the story actually ended. I wanted more."
~**Barnes and Noble reader**

ALSO BY KELLIE COATES GILBERT

Dear Readers,

Thank you for reading this story. If you'd like to read more of my books, please check out these series. To purchase at special discounts: www.kelliecoatesgilbertbooks.com

TETON MOUNTAIN SERIES

Where We Belong – Book 1

Echoes of the Heart – Book 2

Holding the Dream – Book 3

As the Sun Rises – Book 4

Losing the Moon – Book 5

Friends are Forever – Book 6

A Teton Mountain Christmas – Book 7

MAUI ISLAND SERIES

Under the Maui Sky – Book 1

Silver Island Moon – Book 2

Tides of Paradise – Book 3

The Last Aloha – Book 4

Ohana Sunrise – Book 5

Sweet Plumeria Dawn – Book 6

Songs of the Rainbow – Book 7

Hibiscus Christmas – Book 8

PACIFIC BAY SERIES

Chances Are – Book 1

Remember Us – Book 2

Chasing Wind – Book 3

Between Rains – Book 4

SUN VALLEY SERIES

Sisters – Book 1

Heartbeats – Book 2

Changes – Book 3

Promises – Book 4

TEXAS GOLD COLLECTION

A Woman of Fortune – Book 1

Where Rivers Part – Book 2

A Reason to Stay – Book 3

What Matters Most – Book 4

STAND ALONE NOVELS:

Mother of Pearl

AVAILABLE AT ALL MAJOR RETAILERS

FOR EXCLUSIVE DISCOUNTS:

www.kelliecoatesgilbertbooks.com

LOSING THE MOON
TETON MOUNTAIN SERIES, BOOK 5

Kellie Coates Gilbert

1

Distracted, Charlie Grace shut off her computer, thinking there was nothing quieter than late winter snow melting softly outside the cabin's window, weaving rivulets down the panes of glass. She stood and made her way to the opening, peering out at the blurred view of the snow-topped mountains beyond.

In mere minutes, the blanket of gray clouds gave way, and a soft brush of sunshine lit up the frozen white patches scattered among the tufts of vibrant spring grass. The sugar-frosted forest in the distance seemed to lean into the warmth, the deep green pine boughs still glistening with lingering snow as they began to shrug off winter's icy hold. It was as if spring and winter were locked in yet another quarrel, neither willing to yield.

If she had time, she'd grab her camera and try to capture the beauty of it all. Sadly, time was a rare commodity she didn't have a lot of these days. Not with loan renewals, cash flow statements, and tax preparation crowding her task list.

Charlie Grace tore her gaze away from the window and turned back to her desk, where her daunting pile of work awaited her. She barely had a chance to refocus before a movement caught her eye. Startled, she looked up to see Aunt Mo standing in the doorway, casually wiping her hands on a towel.

"Oh, you scared me!" she exclaimed.

Aunt Mo moved into the room. "Didn't mean to, sweetheart." She surveyed the piles of paper next to the computer. "You've been busy."

Charlie Grace slid into her desk chair and nodded as she quickly folded the open bank statement and slid it back into its envelope.

Aunt Mo stepped closer, her gaze roaming over the desk cluttered with papers and landing on the lines of worry that were no doubt etched across Charlie Grace's face. She set the towel on the edge of the desk and leaned one hip against it, crossing her arms.

"You know," she began, her voice soft but steady. "This ranch can be needy. Always wanting more from you than you've got to give."

Charlie Grace let out a faint, distracted laugh, tucking the envelope away into a drawer. "That sounds about right."

Aunt Mo tilted her head, studying her niece. "It's okay to let someone else help carry the load when it gets too heavy. Ranches don't run on sheer willpower alone, honey."

Charlie Grace clenched her jaw, refusing to admit—even to herself—just how hard it had been to keep the ranch afloat over the winter when bills rolled in and income teetered.

Despite a thriving ski season, most tourists lodged in Jackson. She'd lured a few out to the ranch with holiday sleigh rides, but even that was dwindling now that the snowpack was melting and kids were all back in school.

Her bank account showed it.

She looked down, her hands resting on the desk. "I can handle it," she told Aunt Mo, though her voice lacked conviction.

Losing the Moon 3

Aunt Mo smiled gently, reaching out to rest a hand on Charlie Grace's shoulder. "Of course, you can," she said, her tone laced with both pride and quiet understanding. "But handling it doesn't mean you have to do it all alone."

With that, Aunt Mo pushed off the desk and grabbed the towel, flipped it over her shoulder. "Now, I've a pie in the oven, but if you need another set of hands—whether for papers or pies—you know where to find me."

She headed for the door but paused, glancing back over her shoulder. "Just don't wait too long to ask, okay?" Then, with a knowing smile, she disappeared down the hall.

Charlie Grace grabbed her favorite baseball cap off the corner of her desk and placed it on her head, remembering the whirlwind of last summer after her dad had nearly run the place into financial ruin. She'd done everything to transform the struggling cattle operation into a guest ranch. The glossy brochures and promises of adventure had lured visitors in droves, filling the cabins and keeping the dining hall buzzing with laughter.

She'd stepped into the role her father couldn't, quietly negotiating deals, taking on the dirty work, and ensuring every guest left wanting to come back. Saving the ranch wasn't a victory parade; it was a grueling march of determination, and even now, the echoes of those desperate months lingered in the back of her mind.

For a moment, it felt like they'd turned a corner. But as the frozen winter air rolled in, so had the bills—feed, repairs, marketing—and the glaring realization that one stellar season wasn't enough to steady the ship.

A wave of déjà vu washed over her as she stood and peered out the window a second time. She'd been in this exact spot so many months ago, wondering if they'd make it through another year.

The seasons had cycled, but the landscape hadn't changed

—the towering pines, the worn barn, the guest cabins nestled against the foothills—all hauntingly familiar. The stakes were different now, but the weight on her shoulders was the same, as if the past and present had blurred into one relentless cycle of saving what she loved most.

This wasn't just a ranch—it was her legacy, her triumph.

As she turned and headed for the kitchen, she carried with her a mix of pride and pressure. She'd saved the ranch once, and she could do it again.

It was late spring, the mountain tops still snowy white and glistening. Yet, summer was coming, and, with it, the tourist season. Until then, she was ready to roll up her sleeves and find a way to stretch the balance in that bank account somehow.

She really didn't have a choice.

Reva unboxed the pies she'd picked up in Jackson earlier and carefully eased them into the oven to heat. She glanced over her shoulder toward the kitchen window that overlooked the driveway, listening for any signs of her girlfriends arriving early. Satisfied the coast was clear, she folded the empty boxes and shoved them into the back of the pantry behind a row of mismatched jars.

"Out of sight, out of mind," she muttered, brushing her hands together as if that would erase any evidence of her deception.

She retrieved her apron from the hook by the stove and tied it around her waist for good measure. Next, she grabbed a small bowl and poured a bit of flour into it, dusting her hands lightly before swiping them on the apron's front. It wasn't exactly convincing—there weren't any mixing bowls or rolling pins in sight—but it would lend her an air of culinary authenticity if anyone asked.

It wasn't long before the pies began to emit a heavenly scent, the buttery crust mingling with the sweetness of cherries, apples, and pecans. Reva took a deep breath and let herself enjoy the aroma. "If I'd baked these myself, I'd be downright smug," she said with a sly grin.

She set the table with her best dishes and made sure the dessert forks sparkled under the light. When she heard laughter and approaching footsteps, she quickly positioned herself by the counter, wiping an imaginary streak of sweat from her forehead.

There was a quick knock, and the door swung open. Capri was the first to saunter in, followed by Charlie Grace and Lila. "Smells amazing in here!" Capri exclaimed, tossing her jacket over the back of a chair.

"Homemade pie," Reva said nonchalantly, waving a hand toward the oven. "Been at it all afternoon."

Lila raised an eyebrow, stepping closer. "You've been baking? Between chasing after little Lucan and managing the town's affairs, when do you even have the time?"

Reva laughed nervously and shooed them toward the table. "A woman has to have her secrets."

Charlie Grace leaned against the counter, a teasing smile playing on her lips as she watched Reva take the pies from the oven. "Hmm, let me guess—Tillman's Bakery in Jackson? Their pies have that unmistakable crust pattern."

Reva froze but quickly recovered, waving a dish towel in Charlie Grace's direction. "Oh, stop. Don't you have a hunky new boyfriend to focus on? I heard he took a trip back to California."

Charlie Grace shrugged. "Yeah, he's in L.A. this week. Some post-Oscar event. I'm learning schmoozing is about half of his job when he's not filming."

Reva picked up a knife and began cutting into the cherry pie. "Networking is important." She paused, considering whether to come clean. Finally, her guilt got the best of her. "Okay, okay. I didn't make the pies. I just...baked them. But I did make the chocolate martinis." She tilted her head in the direction of her own glass. "And my mocha milk."

Capri chuckled, taking a seat. "Ha, the truth comes out. If they taste half as good as they smell, I don't care where they came from."

"I agree," Lila said, picking up a fork. "I like two kinds of pies...hot and cold."

Charlie Grace raised an eyebrow while pointing. "So, the flour on your apron was just for show?"

"Exactly. I'm a visionary, not a baker." Reva waved her fork like a wand. "Besides, those bakery pies are better than anything I could whip up, and they don't come with the risk of a fire alarm."

Lila shook her head, laughing as she reached for another slice. "You're shameless."

"Absolutely," Reva said, popping a bite into her mouth. "And you love me for it."

Charlie Grace caught her eye with a knowing smirk. "Sure, Reva. Whatever you say." She turned to Lila. "What do you hear from your daughter? How's school?"

Immediately, a wide grin broke out on Lila's face.

"What?" asked Charlie Grace.

"It's hard not to smile. Camille is loving it at the university. She's made friends and is taking a full load of classes she seems to be acing." Her voice drifted slightly. "She's living what I've always wanted for her."

Reva picked up her glass of mocha milk. "You've done a fine job, Lila. I'm learning parenting is hard on so many levels. I can't imagine doing it as a single mother."

She eyed Capri. "What's up with you? You look like you just won the lottery or something."

Capri leaned back in her chair, her fork idly pushing

crumbs around her dessert plate. "Nothing much," she began, a mischievous glint in her eye, "Only that I signed up for the snowmobile race next weekend."

The room went silent, forks paused mid-air. Charlie Grace was the first to break the silence. "Wait. The one up on Devil's Staircase?"

"That's the one," Capri said, a satisfied grin spreading across her face. "Racers from multiple states will be competing. I'll be one of them."

Reva's jaw dropped. "Capri! You know that area's a death-trap this time of year! The avalanche warnings have been off the charts."

"Warnings, schwarnings," Capri said with a dismissive wave of her hand. "It's fine. I know the terrain like the back of my hand."

Lila narrowed her eyes, crossing her arms. "Knowing the terrain doesn't make you immune to a thirty-ton wall of snow coming down the mountain."

Capri rolled her eyes. "They always set off blasts prior to the race to trigger possible slides. I'm not worried."

"But, what if—" Lila argued.

"Lila, if I listened to every 'what if,' I'd never leave the house." Capri leaned forward, her voice growing animated. "This is going to be epic! Snow flying everywhere, engines roaring, the wind in your face—freedom!"

Charlie Grace gave her a pointed look. "Freedom? You mean freezing."

Capri laughed, brushing off the concern. "Oh, come on! What's the point of living if you don't push yourself every now and then? Besides, I've got the best sled in the race. Bodhi tuned it up, and I'll be fine."

"Capri." Reva crossed her arms, the tone in her voice firm. "This isn't about how good your snowmobile is. Unexpected avalanches don't check your equipment before they barrel down the mountain. They're dangerous, unpredictable, and they don't give second chances."

Lila raised an eyebrow. "And what does Jake think about all this?"

Capri let out an exaggerated sigh and rolled her eyes. "Jake is wonderful, but he's not my keeper. He doesn't get a vote on how I spend my weekends. Besides, you're all acting like this is my first brush with adrenaline. Need I remind you of the class five rapids I tackled last spring? Solo, might I add."

Charlie Grace shook her head with a groan. "And we're still recovering from the emotional trauma of that one."

Capri smirked, unrepentant. "It was incredible. You should try it sometime—gets the heart racing in all the right ways."

"Yeah, like straight into cardiac arrest," Reva shot back. "You keep tempting fate, Capri. One of these days, it might actually answer."

"I agree. That rafting stunt was reckless," Charlie Grace muttered.

"And awesome," Capri shot back. "Look, I get it. You're all worried. But I'm not scared of a little snow. The sponsors will take every safety precaution. If I win—and I will—you can all sit back and say you know the champion of Devil's Staircase."

Reva groaned, putting her head in her hands. "You're impossible."

"Maybe," Capri said, grabbing the last bite of pie. "But I'm also fun, and that counts for something."

Lila shook her head, a small smile tugging at her lips. "If fun gets you buried under six feet of snow, don't say we didn't warn you."

Capri raised her fork like a toast. "Noted. Now, pass the whipped cream. I'll need the fuel."

2

Charlie Grace arrived home to a quiet house. Her dad was already in bed and Jewel was spending the night over at Gibbs' house. Her ex-husband's yellow lab had puppies and Jewel was enamored. Her daughter had already named all of them and was determined to talk her into letting her bring at least one home with her.

"Sorry, baby," Charlie Grace had told her. "We have enough animals to feed. You're just going to have to spend time with the puppies over at your dad's house."

The click of the bedroom door closing behind her offered a momentary retreat from the chaos of the day. As she slipped into her nighttime routine, she realized she hadn't heard from Nick all day. Typically, he texted at least once a day, if not multiple times. She opened her phone and checked to be sure she hadn't missed a message, but the screen remained stubbornly blank.

With a sigh, she plugged her phone into the charger and slipped into her favorite flannel pajamas, the kind a woman chooses when she's divorced, home alone, and her boyfriend is out of town.

As Charlie Grace climbed into bed, she found herself staring at the ceiling, her thoughts circling around how lucky she was to have found Nick. His life as a production designer often pulled him back to Los Angeles, where the demands of his career were rooted in a world so different from Thunder Mountain. Even though he'd sold his house and moved closer to be with her, the travel remained constant—a reminder that, no matter how much he loved her, part of his heart belonged to his work.

With a restless sigh, Charlie Grace sat up in bed and reached for her laptop on the nightstand. If sleep wasn't coming easily, she might as well distract herself. Flipping open the top, the familiar glow of the screen filled the room as she logged in and navigated to her social media.

Nick's social media was filled with snapshots from the Oscars—a glittering world far removed from her rustic life on the ranch. There he was, smiling in his tuxedo, standing alongside stunning actresses draped in couture gowns that shimmered like starlight.

Charlie Grace had never cared much for Hollywood's glitz and pretense but seeing him surrounded by so much beauty and sophistication stirred an old insecurity deep inside her. What could a woman in dusty boots and flannel shirts really offer a man accustomed to red carpets and designer dresses?

Charlie Grace thought of her parents' marriage, a union that had weathered its share of storms—a few bad ones—but always held firm. Her mother and father had faced financial struggles, health scares, and the exhausting demands of raising a child with an independent streak, yet their commitment to each other never wavered.

She'd been young when her mother died but remembered there was something steady and reassuring about the way they loved—built not on grand gestures but on countless small acts of loyalty and care. Her dad's soft chuckle when her mom teased him about his favorite chair, the way her mom drew his hot bath every night even after decades together—it all spoke of a bond forged through time and trust.

Charlie Grace had always longed for that kind of relationship, one that could stand the test of hardship and change.

She and Nick had been together for about nine months now. They'd first crossed paths when he stayed at the ranch as a guest, their shared love of photography sparking an instant connection. That spark had grown into a deeper connection, a bond that felt both steady and exhilarating.

Nick was everything she hadn't found in her past relationships—confident, adventurous, and brimming with passion for life. He made her feel seen in a way no one else ever had. Her former boyfriend, Jason, had been dependable but uninspired, his presence fading quietly into the background of her life. And her ex-husband, Gibbs? He had a knack for excuses and a wandering eye that made loving him feel like chasing the wind—futile and exhausting.

Her track record with love was far from perfect, but that didn't stop her from longing for something lasting. The idea of a true partnership—someone to share the quiet evenings and life's big moments—had always tugged at her heart. And now, with Jewel growing up so quickly, the thought of growing old alone loomed larger than ever.

As much as she valued her independence, the idea of facing the years ahead without someone by her side unsettled her. For the first time in years, she allowed herself to wonder—could Nick be that person? And perhaps the bigger question—could she let herself believe in forever again?

∽

Reva leaned against the kitchen counter, the faint laughter of her girlfriends still echoing in her ears as she rinsed the last of the martini glasses. The evening had been a perfect blend of banter, heartfelt confessions, and a sprinkling of ridiculous jokes that left her smiling long after the door closed behind the last of her friends.

Truth was, she cherished these women like sisters, their bond forged through decades of shared laughter, heartaches, and triumphs. They had seen each other through every season of life—first loves, shattered dreams, weddings, and babies—and no matter how busy or complicated things became, they were her constant, her safe place. To Reva, they weren't just friends; they were family, the kind she chose and would fiercely protect, no matter what.

The sound of the front door creaking open made her pause mid-motion, a smile already forming. The familiar rumble of Kellen's voice and Lucan's gleeful giggles spilled into the entryway, filling the house with a warmth she hadn't realized she'd been missing all evening.

"We're back!" Kellen called, carrying a very sleepy, but still wriggling, Lucan in his arms.

Reva set the glass down and turned toward them with a smile. "Did you have fun at the hockey rink, buddy?"

Lucan's face lit up as Kellen set him down, his little legs wobbling with excitement. "Mama! I skate! I go fast!" he said, running while holding his arms out like airplane wings.

"And Daddy hold me! I not fall—'cept one time." He scrunched his nose in concentration, then broke into a giggle. "Ice so slippy!"

"It was awesome," Kellen confirmed, grinning. "This kid's got a future on the ice. He's likely to have a slapshot that'll knock your socks off."

Reva ruffled Lucan's dark curls and kissed his forehead. "I'm so glad you boys had fun. You're amazing, Lucan. But I think it's time to get you ready for bed. What do you say?"

Lucan yawned dramatically and rested his head against Kellen's knee. "Tuck me in, Mommy."

Contentment washed over Reva as they headed upstairs together. After a quick bedtime story about a daring moose and his snowy adventures, Reva pulled the blankets up to Lucan's chin and kissed his cheek. "Sweet dreams, my little champion."

"Night, Mommy. Night, Daddy," Lucan mumbled, already drifting off.

In their bedroom, Reva tugged off her earrings and set them on the dresser while Kellen peeled off his sweater, tossing it into the laundry basket.

"Thanks for taking our son out tonight," Reva said, disrobing. "I think he really needed it. He has so much energy and being cooped up in this house all winter hasn't been easy."

"He wasn't the only one who needed it," Kellen teased, a knowing smile tugging at his lips. "How was your girls' night?"

"Good," Reva said, pausing as she reached for her moisturizer. "But I'm a little worried about Capri. She's signed up for this snowmobile race next weekend, and you know how unpredictable the mountains can be this time of year. Avalanches, hidden obstacles—she's fearless to a fault."

Kellen stepped closer, placing his hands on her shoulders and squeezing gently. "Capri's a grown woman, Reva. She knows the risks, and you can't keep her from living her life."

"I know," Reva admitted, her voice tinged with reluctance. "It's just...I feel like I've always been the one to keep us all together, to look out for them when they can't see what's coming."

Kellen raised an eyebrow as he sat down on the edge of the bed. "Always? Even back in your rebellious, Doc Martens-wearing, late-to-class high school days?"

She laughed softly, sitting beside him. "No Doc Martens for

this group. Only hiking boots or Tony Lama cowboy boots." She paused thoughtfully. "Except for me, Nike Air Force 1 was my shoe of choice."

Kellen smiled, his eyes softening. "Guess even back then, you were marching to your own beat." He tilted her chin toward him with a gentle hand. "And now you're the heart of this family. But you can't be everything to everyone, Reva. You've got to trust your friends to take care of themselves sometimes."

She sighed, leaning her head against his shoulder. "You're right. I know you're right. I just...can't help it."

"Good thing I married a woman with such a big heart," Kellen murmured, his lips brushing her temple. "Now, let's see if I can distract you from saving the world for a little while."

Reva laughed as he eased her back onto the bed, his hands warm and insistent on her waist. "You always have a personal agenda, don't you?"

"Only when it comes to you," he said, grinning as he leaned in to kiss her.

LILA TURNED onto her quiet street, her shoulders heavy with the weariness of a long day at the clinic. The temptation to skip tonight's girlfriend gathering had tugged at her earlier, but she knew better than to even suggest it. Reva would have none of that—these nights were sacred, a lifeline they all clung to in the rush of their busy lives.

The snow clung stubbornly to the curbs, piled high from last week's storm, but the clear sky gave her a momentary sense of calm. The sight of her little house at the end of the block was always a welcome reprieve. She glanced up at the front porch as she approached, her headlights sweeping over the steps.

Someone was there.

Her heart skipped a beat. She slowed the truck, eyes narrowing, then her stomach dropped as recognition hit.

Camille?

Slamming the truck into park, Lila yanked her keys from the ignition and hurried out, the icy wind cutting through her coat. Camille sat on the top step, bundled in a thick down parka, her knees pulled to her chest. Her head was bowed, but Lila didn't miss the telltale shake of her shoulders. She was shivering.

"Camille!" Lila's voice rose above the crunch of her boots on the snow-packed driveway. "What are you doing here? Why are you sitting outside? Where's your key?"

Camille flinched at her mother's voice, looking up with a faint, apologetic smile. "I couldn't find it," she said, her voice hoarse and trembling. "I…I thought I had it, but…I didn't."

Lila frowned, climbing the steps two at a time. Up close, Camille's cheeks were flushed from the cold, her eyes shadowed and tired. "How long have you been out here?" Lila demanded, wrapping her arm around Camille's shoulders and pulling her close. "It's freezing!"

"Not long," Camille mumbled, though her stiff body suggested otherwise.

Lila glanced around, confused. "Where's your car? And why didn't you call me?"

Lila didn't waste another moment waiting for answers. She fumbled with her keys, fingers clumsy in her gloves, and threw the door open. The rush of warmth hit them like a wave, and Lila quickly ushered Camille inside.

"Sit down," Lila instructed, her tone clipped as she helped her daughter out of her parka. She hung it on the hook by the door, glancing over her shoulder to see Camille sink onto the couch, her shoulders slumped. Something was wrong. That much was clear.

"You could've called me," Lila said as she moved toward the

kitchen to start the kettle. Her voice softened slightly, though her worry bubbled just beneath the surface. "I would've come home right away. Why didn't you call?" she repeated.

"I didn't want to bother you," Camille replied, her tone faint and uneven. "And my car is back at school. I caught a ride with...a friend."

Lila paused, hands gripping the counter, before turning to face her daughter. "You never bother me. You know that. Now, what's going on? Why are you here? Why aren't you at school?"

Camille hesitated, her gaze fixed on her hands, which were fidgeting nervously in her lap. Lila's heart clenched. The silence stretched, thick and heavy, until Camille finally looked up.

"I needed to talk to you," she said, her voice cracking.

Lila crossed the room, sitting down beside Camille. She reached out, placing a hand on her daughter's knee. "Okay," she said, keeping her voice steady. "Then talk to me. What's going on?"

Camille took a shaky breath, her eyes glistening. "I—I'm moving home."

Lila blinked, the words not quite registering. She felt the floor tilt beneath her, though she tried to keep her expression calm. "Moving home?" she repeated slowly. "What do you mean? You've only been at the university for a semester. I thought things were going well."

"I thought so, too," Camille admitted, her voice a whisper. Her hands twisted together until the knuckles turned white. "But...things got complicated. I—I couldn't stay."

"Complicated how?" Lila pressed, her mind racing. Camille had seemed fine during their last phone call—busy with classes, making friends, settling into campus life. Now, looking at her daughter's pale, drawn face, she realized how much Camille had kept hidden.

Camille swallowed hard, her gaze darting to the floor.

"Mom," she began, her voice trembling. "There's...there's something I need to tell you. Something important."

Lila's breath caught. She wasn't sure what she was expecting, but the weight in Camille's tone told her it wasn't going to be easy. "Whatever it is, you can tell me," she said softly, squeezing her daughter's knee.

Camille's eyes filled with tears, and she let out a shaky exhale. "I'm pregnant."

3

The shop smelled of oil, grease, and the faint metallic tang of machinery. Capri knelt beside her Arctic Cat ZR1000 snowmobile, a wrench in her hand as she tweaked the motor with practiced precision. The hum of the fluorescent lights overhead barely registered as she focused on the fine adjustments. Her whitewater business might be her bread and butter, but this—working with her hands, tweaking engines—this was her escape.

Bodhi West leaned against the workbench behind her, his lanky frame casually draped over the edge as he watched her work. "You sure about this race, Capri?" he asked, his tone light but carrying an undercurrent of concern. "I've heard it can get pretty gnarly, especially this time of year. Spring melt, chance of avalanches..."

Capri glanced up, arching an eyebrow. A smirk played on her lips. "You getting soft on me, Bodhi? I thought you were the king of adrenaline around here."

He chuckled. "I like a good rush, sure. But I also like keeping my limbs intact. Just saying, the Tetons don't always play nice."

Before Capri could respond, the shop door swung open with a burst of cold air, and a woman's voice rang out. "Hey, Bodhi!" Alyssa, Bodhi's girlfriend, strode in, her cheeks pink from the chill and her arms wrapped tightly around her midsection. "You need to come home and take a shower before we head to Jackson. And we still need to pick a movie."

Bodhi sighed dramatically, his good-natured annoyance evident. "What's on the list this time?"

Alyssa's eyes lit up as she rattled off titles. "There's *The Notebook, Crazy Rich Asians,* and *Pride and Prejudice!* They all look so good!"

Bodhi pinched the bridge of his nose as if physically pained. "What about *John Wick* or *Top Gun: Maverick*? Something with explosions, you know? High stakes?"

Alyssa gasped in mock offense. "Bodhi West, how dare you! Romance movies are high stakes! You've got people risking it all for love. And you *cried* during *Titanic,* so don't even try to act tough."

Bodhi rolled his eyes but couldn't keep the grin off his face. "Fine. *Crazy Rich Asians,* but I'm picking the snacks."

She squealed, throwing her arms around his neck and pressing a quick kiss to his cheek. "You're the best!" She patted him on the behind before turning for the door. "See you at home," she called over her shoulder as she disappeared into the cold.

Capri leaned back on her heels and slipped her torque wrench into her back pocket. "You're such a pushover, Bodhi."

He shrugged, his gaze lingering on the door Alyssa had just exited. "Relationships aren't about keeping score, Capri. Sometimes, giving in is the win."

Capri snorted softly. "Spoken like a guy who just lost the argument. Now, go grab me a spare package of spark plugs before you start sounding like a romance movie yourself."

Bodhi laughed, heading toward the shelves crammed with

parts. As he scanned the cluttered space, something bright caught his eye—a vase of artificial sunflowers perched incongruously between oil filters and old manuals. He paused, his brow furrowing slightly, before reaching for the spark plugs.

"What?" Capri asked.

Bodhi shrugged. "It's just...you don't often see flowers in a shop. Especially your shop."

"So what? I have an affinity for sunflowers. Not a crime," she challenged.

Bodhi tucked a smile away. No doubt, Jake had something to do with it. That guy seemed to bring out Capri's softer side. But he knew better than to say so to her. Not if he wanted to have a hind end left to sit on.

Capri tightened the last bolt on the engine. Bodhi turned up the radio, and the announcer's voice filled the room. "Snow is on its way, folks—a little early spring surprise, but not uncommon in the Tetons. Stay safe out there!"

Capri straightened, shutting the snowmobile's top with a satisfying clunk. "There we go. She's ready for the big race."

Bodhi handed her the spark plugs and watched as she tucked them in the sled's storage compartment. "I'll clean up the tools," he said, gathering them off the concrete floor.

Capri wiped her hands on a mechanic's towel and headed to the door, pulling it open to step into the crisp air. Snowflakes danced on the breeze, and across the road, a moose stood motionless, its dark form outlined against the trees, steam rising faintly from its nose.

"Wow," Bodhi whispered from behind her. "Look at that."

Capri folded her arms, watching the snow gather on the moose's broad back. "New snow," she murmured, a faint smile tugging at her lips. The flakes drifted softly, silently, but the shiver that ran through her had nothing to do with the cold. The Devil's Staircase race was right around the corner, and she could already taste the thrill of victory.

4

Morning dawned gray and heavy with snow, muffling the world beyond the windows. Lila pulled herself from the warmth of her bed, her body heavy with fatigue after a sleepless night of tossing and turning. Her thoughts had spun relentlessly, tangling themselves in the ramifications of Camille's situation and the night before.

Lila's daughter's words had hit like a thunderclap, leaving Lila momentarily stunned. Her hand fell away from Camille's knee as her mind scrambled to catch up. *Pregnant.* Her daughter—her Camille—was pregnant. She searched Camille's face for some hint that this was a mistake or a misunderstanding, but all she saw was raw vulnerability.

For a moment, neither of them spoke. The space had felt too small, the silence deafening. Lila finally found her voice, though it was barely above a whisper.

"How far along are you?" she'd asked, her throat tight.

"Almost three months," Camille said, her voice breaking.

Camille's dating life had always been a carousel of flashing smiles and fleeting connections, each boy just another painted horse vying for his turn. The ride spun on, but none stayed long—which was exactly how Camille wanted it.

Lila had looked to the star-filled sky and let out a painful breath while trying to process. "Who's the father? Does he know?"

Camille shook her head quickly. "No. And he's not going to. He...he's not someone I want in my life, or the baby's."

"Oh, honey. I'm not sure that's your choice. The father has a right to—"

"Mom, back off."

The harsh reply stung a little. Still, Lila's chest ached as she looked at her daughter, who suddenly seemed so much younger, so fragile. She reached out, taking Camille's hands in her own. "We'll figure this out," she'd said, her voice steady despite the storm of emotions swirling inside her. "We'll figure everything out."

Camille's tears spilled over, and she nodded, her grip tightening on Lila's hands. "I'm sorry, Mom," she whispered. "About all of it."

Lila shook her head, swallowing her disappointment. "Don't apologize. We'll get through this. Together."

But as she'd held her daughter close, her mind raced with questions and fears she wasn't ready to voice. Together or not, their lives had just changed forever.

Lila then spent the night staring at the bedroom ceiling, her arms aching with the memory of holding Camille, while her mind spiraled through an endless maze of what-ifs. The enormity of what lay ahead pressed down on her chest, demanding answers she didn't have. She couldn't yet see the shape of their future, only the jagged edges of the unknown—and the sharp reality that some pieces might never fit together the way she hoped.

Financial worries gnawed at her—the assistance she'd lined up for her daughter's schooling could evaporate now. She could manage without it, of course, but at what cost? Would her focus falter under the weight of it all? And how would she navigate the potential awkwardness of running into the young man responsible for this upheaval?

She now padded to the kitchen, careful not to make noise. Camille's door remained firmly shut, and Lila didn't want to disturb her. She needed answers, but not at the expense of their relationship. Camille had always trusted her, but Lila knew instinctively that pressing too hard now could push her away. Camille would open up when she was ready.

Still, how could she let her return to school? The thought of her daughter being hours away during this pregnancy—it was unbearable. Lila's chest tightened as she thought of her own lonely pregnancy, relying on letters and sporadic calls from Fallujah to feel connected to her husband. Camille would need her now more than ever.

Lila moved with practiced quiet, setting the kettle to boil and spooning grounds into the French press. The snow outside reflected pale light into the kitchen as she retrieved her favorite mug, the one with a crack along the handle that had somehow held firm for years. Her hands shook as she poured the steaming water over the coffee grounds, and the tears came silently, slipping down her cheeks as she stared out into the storm.

She whispered into the stillness, her voice trembling as she spoke to her long-dead husband. "Oh, Aaron...what do I do? Our daughter needs me, but I don't even know how to help her yet. I wish you were here. You'd know what to say."

The sound of the kettle clicking off punctuated her grief, and she wiped her face with the back of her hand as if erasing the evidence. Just then, the phone rang, startling her. She grabbed it quickly, glancing at Camille's closed door.

"Hello?"

"Morning, Lila," came Reva's familiar, cheerful tone. "Just

checking—are we still on for delivering meals today? Roads are messy, but we've got a snowstorm crew ready to go."

Lila cleared her throat, forcing a casual tone. "I may have had a change of plans."

"Oh?" came Reva's reply, not so easily fooled. "What's up?"

Lila had a quick change of heart, not ready to invite questions...or provide answers she didn't have. "Never mind. I'll be ready in an hour."

In the background, she heard Camille stirring upstairs. When she poked her head out moments later and descended the staircase, Lila covered the mouthpiece of the phone. "Camille, I committed to help deliver meals."

Camille hesitated, the faintest flush creeping up her neck. "It's no problem, Mom. Go—I have some studying to do."

Lila caught the flicker of something behind her daughter's eyes but let it pass. "We'll talk more when I get home, okay?" She watched as her daughter grabbed her backpack, retreated back to her room, and shut the door.

"Who are you talking to?" Reva asked when Lila returned to the conversation.

"Uh, no one," Lila replied, perhaps a touch too quickly. "Just the dog. I'll see you soon."

She hung up before more questions could come and stood there for a moment, gripping the counter. Then she heard it—the crunch of tires in the snow. She glanced out the window and saw a familiar truck pulling up. Whit Calloway.

A minute later, Whit was on the porch, chains slung over one shoulder and an easy smile on his face. He stamped snow off his boots before stepping inside, the smell of cold clinging to him.

"Thought you might need these," he said, holding up the chains. "Roads are slick."

Lila shook her head, smiling despite herself. "This is spring snow, Whit. It never sticks. Gone by noon."

Her friend shrugged. "Better safe than sorry."

Lila studied him for a moment, his presence somehow grounding her. She didn't feel quite as overwhelmed with him standing there. She offered him coffee, and he accepted with a grin. "Just let me get these on first."

Whit strode across the driveway and to her car, chains slung over his shoulder, his breath visible in the crisp mountain air. Lila stood on the porch, her arms wrapped around herself against the chill, watching him work. For a fleeting moment, the weight on her chest felt just a little lighter.

"There, all done," he said when he'd finished. He smiled with that quiet, familiar grin he seemed to reserve just for her. He climbed the steps, brushing the snow off his hands. "That should do it."

"Thanks," Lila said, brushing her fingers against his. The touch lingered, just long enough to send a flicker of heat through her. "You didn't have to do this."

"I wanted to," he replied, leaning in slightly. "Plus, I like having excuses to see you."

Lila smiled, but her gaze drifted toward the window upstairs, where she could just barely make out the corner of Camille's curtain. The tension in her chest tightened, and Whit noticed.

"What's wrong?" he asked, his tone low.

"Camille's home," Lila said quietly. "She's upstairs."

Whit straightened, the easy smile fading into something more careful. "Didn't realize she'd be here."

"She came back last night. Surprise visit." Lila tried to sound light, but it came out strained. "She doesn't know you're here."

Whit tilted his head, studying her. "You want me to leave?"

"No," she said quickly, her hand reaching for his arm. "I just...wasn't expecting her, that's all."

He nodded, his expression softening. "Everything alright?" he gently probed.

"Not really," Lila murmured.

He followed her inside, his movements deliberate, like he was giving her space. Her chest ached at how understanding he always was.

Whit leaned against the counter, arms crossed, as Lila moved around the kitchen. The low hum of the kettle on the stove filled the silence between them. He'd shown up to bring the chains for her car, but somehow they'd ended up here, in the warmth of the kitchen, with something much heavier hanging in the air.

Lila stood by the sink, staring out the window at the frost formed on the grass. She gripped the edge of the counter, as if steadying herself for what she was about to say.

"Camille's pregnant," she said softly, her voice barely audible over the hum of the refrigerator.

Whit straightened, his eyes searching hers. "What?"

"She told me last night," Lila continued, turning to face him. Her arms crossed protectively over her chest. "She's scared. I'm scared. I don't even know what to say to her, let alone what to do."

Whit stayed quiet for a moment, letting the weight of her words settle. Then, he stepped closer, his boots scuffing softly against the tiled floor. "How's she handling it?"

Lila let out a shaky breath. "Not great. She's overwhelmed. She hasn't told anyone else yet—just me. And I...I don't think I've been handling it very well either." She looked down, her voice breaking. "She's so young, Whit. This isn't what I wanted for her. Not like this."

Whit reached out, his hand warm as it covered hers on the counter. "Lila, it's okay to feel that way. It's a lot to take in."

She looked up at him, her eyes shining with unshed tears.

"What if I fail her? What if I don't know how to help her through this?"

"You won't fail," Whit said firmly, his gaze steady. "You're her mom. You've been there for her through everything, and you'll be there for her now. She's lucky to have you."

Lila gave a hollow laugh, brushing at her cheek. "I don't feel like enough right now. Goodness, I don't even have all the information, let alone answers. I didn't want to push."

"You don't have to have all the answers," he said gently. "Just be there. That's what she needs most."

She searched his face, the warmth and understanding in his eyes easing some of the tension in her chest. "I guess we'll get through this. We don't have a choice."

"I know you can," Whit said. "And if you need me—if Camille needs me—I'm here. For both of you."

The tears spilled over then, and she let out a soft, broken laugh. "You make it sound so simple."

"It's not simple," he admitted, his voice softening. "But you're not alone, Lila. You've got me. And together, we'll figure it out."

For a long moment, she just stood there, letting his words settle into the parts of her heart that had been clenched with fear and doubt. She nodded, swallowing hard. "Thank you," she whispered.

For years after losing Aaron, she'd had to carry every heavy weight on her shoulders...alone. It felt odd to have a man to share the burdens. It felt good.

He pulled her into his arms, and she let herself sink into the solid comfort of him, the smell of leather and cedar grounding her. For the first time since Camille had dropped the news, she felt like she could breathe again.

As they stood there in the quiet kitchen, the kettle's whistle fading into the background, a sound from upstairs broke the moment—Camille's footsteps on the stairs.

Lila pulled back, wiping at her face. "That's her," she said, her voice low.

Whit nodded. "Do you want me to go?" he offered.

Lila looked at him, her heart swelling with gratitude and something deeper, something steady and certain. She reached for his hand, squeezing it tightly as Camille's hesitant figure appeared in the doorway.

"Hey," Camille said softly, her eyes darting between them.

"Hey," Lila replied, her voice steady now. "We were just talking about you."

Camille froze, her expression uncertain, but Whit's warm smile and gentle nod seemed to ease some of her tension. "We're here for you, Camille," he said simply.

Lila glanced at him, the weight of his words settling over all three of them. As Camille stepped further into the kitchen, Lila realized they weren't just navigating a new chapter—they were building something stronger, together.

As the coffee steamed in her hands, Lila's thoughts caught up with the moment.

I'm going to be a grandmother.

The words echoed in her mind, strange and surreal, like trying on a coat two sizes too big. Her grip tightened on the mug as a mix of awe and panic swirled inside her. She bit back the urge to say anything, to fill the space with her usual wit. Instead, she let the realization settle in.

And for the first time in a long while, she wasn't sure whether to laugh, cry, or do both at once.

5

Days later, Capri pulled her Dodge D150 Adventurer 'Lil Red Express into the parking lot at the base of Devil's Staircase. The truck, gleaming in its signature red with chrome stacks, looked every bit as proud and polished as its owner. Capri cut the engine and hopped out, her boots crunching on the packed snow. Despite the crisp morning air, her breath puffed steadily as she moved to the trailer hitched behind the truck.

Bodhi was already there, tugging at the straps that held Capri's snowmobile in place. His lanky frame was bundled up against the cold in a faded REI jacket and snow pants that had seen better days. "You weren't kidding about babying this truck," he said, casting an admiring glance at the Dodge. "It's cleaner than my kitchen."

Capri smirked. "Don't go comparing my truck to whatever disaster zone you call a kitchen. This beauty deserves respect." She climbed up to assist him, unhooking the straps with quick precision. Together, they eased the snowmobile down from the trailer. The sled gleamed as brightly as the truck, its polished surface reflecting the white expanse around them.

The parking lot buzzed with activity. Other racers were unloading their own sleds, laughing and joking as they prepared for the grueling backcountry race ahead. The rumble of engines echoed off the canyon walls, mixing with the occasional cheer or bark of a dog. Capri took it all in, her adrenaline already starting to hum.

She turned her gaze to the Devil's Staircase trailhead, the course's infamous starting point. The course loomed ahead, winding up a narrow path that seemed to claw its way toward the sky. From this vantage, it looked almost innocent, a gentle incline cushioned by freshly fallen snow. But Capri knew better. Just past that first deceptive stretch, the trail would rear up with a thousand-foot elevation gain over a single brutal mile.

The Devil's Staircase was the kind of place that could break you if you weren't careful. Nestled deep in Teton Canyon on the Idaho side of the mountain range, it was often overshadowed by the more famous Alaska Basin and Table Mountain trails. But what the Devil's Staircase lacked in renown, it made up for in raw, untamed beauty. She could see the jagged edges of the canyon walls cutting sharply into the pale morning sky; their rugged lines softened slightly by snow. Somewhere up there, unique vistas waited, views she'd never forget if she could manage to reach them.

"You ready for this?" Bodhi asked, breaking into her thoughts.

Capri glanced at him, her dark eyes flashing with determination. "Born ready."

He laughed, shaking his head. "You're crazy, you know that? Racing Devil's Staircase? Half these guys won't even finish."

"Then it'll just make it that much sweeter when I do." She pulled her helmet out of the cab and snapped it into place, her voice muffled but no less sure. "Let's get this beast warmed up."

Bodhi gave her a mock salute and stepped back as Capri

straddled the snowmobile. The engine roared to life beneath her, a powerful sound that sent vibrations humming through her legs and chest. She gave it a quick rev, a grin spreading across her face.

This was her domain—challenging, unpredictable, and demanding her full focus. The kind of place where she could lose herself and find herself all at once. Capri tightened her grip on the handlebars, her pulse quickening as she stared up at the challenge ahead. Devil's Staircase was waiting, and she couldn't wait to meet it head-on.

As she maneuvered her snowmobile toward the line-up area, a flash of movement caught her eye. Turning her head, Capri saw Charlie Grace's old pickup rumble into the lot, joining other spectators from town. The familiar sight of her friend's truck made her pause, a smile tugging at her lips. In the cab, Capri could make out Lila and Reva squeezed in next to Charlie Grace, all bundled up in winter coats. After parking, they climbed out. When they spotted her, all three women waved enthusiastically, their gloved hands flapping like flags against the backdrop of the snowy canyon.

Capri waved back, feeling a warmth that had nothing to do with the engine's heat. It meant something to see them here, braving the cold to support her. Despite their worry and dire warnings, they showed up. And that was enough to steady her nerves and bolster her confidence. With a nod to herself, Capri refocused on the race ahead. It was time to prove what she was made of.

Bodhi held up a handheld radio to his mouth, pointing to her helmet.

Capri nodded and switched on the radio receiver in her helmet.

"Go get 'em," Bodhi urged with a wide grin. "You got this."

She gave him a quick thumbs-up. Her pulse quickened with anticipation as she maneuvered to join the other racers at the starting gate, the roar of engines and smell of oil sharpening her focus. Her hands gripped the handlebars of her snowmobile tightly and waited.

The air was crisp and biting, the kind of cold that stung her cheeks and turned her breath into plumes of fog. Around her, the low rumble of engines filled the still morning, a growling prelude to the chaos about to erupt. To her left, a wiry man with a jagged scar across his cheek revved his engine, sneering in her direction. To her right, a teenager barely out of high school bounced in his seat, a nervous grin plastered on his face.

Ahead of them, the race marshal, bundled in a thick parka, climbed onto a small platform. He held a starter pistol aloft, its sleek black barrel gleaming under the weak winter sun. The racers tensed, their engines roaring louder, echoing through the valley like the rumble of distant thunder. Capri's heart pounded in rhythm with the machine beneath her, the vibration coursing through her like an electric current.

"Racers, ready!" the marshal shouted into the microphone, his voice carrying over the din.

Capri shifted in her seat, her gloved fingers tightening their grip as she leaned forward, her entire body coiled like a spring. The world around her seemed to fade, narrowing to the path ahead.

The marshal pulled the trigger. A sharp crack split the air, and the blank discharged into the sky.

Twenty snowmobiles surged forward in a synchronized burst of power and fury, engines roaring in an earsplitting crescendo. The track beneath them was packed snow, groomed just enough to hold the weight of the machines. Red tape fluttered on stakes marking the initial half mile of the course. Capri tore down the straightaway, her snowmobile responding to every slight adjustment with precision.

Even through her helmet, the wind howled in her ears, and the roar of the machines was deafening. Adrenaline surged through her veins, her pulse a rapid staccato beat. This was what she lived for—the speed, the danger, the utter freedom of being in control of her own fate. She leaned into the handlebars, her eyes narrowing as she scanned the path ahead.

THE RED TAPE disappeared as the racers veered off the marked course and into the uncharted wilderness of Devil's Staircase. The landscape morphed into a chaotic blur of jagged rocks, towering pines, and icy patches. Capri swerved sharply to avoid a low-hanging branch, cutting in front of another racer in the process. The man yelled something she couldn't hear over the cacophony of engines, and she smirked beneath her helmet.

She powered through a steep incline, her snowmobile bucking beneath her as it climbed over uneven ground. The machine's suspension groaned but held steady. Ahead, a jagged outcrop of rocks loomed, and Capri barely had time to react. She shifted her weight, the snowmobile's skis lifting off the ground as she cleared the obstacle with a bone-jarring jolt. Her heart leapt into her throat, and she let out a whoop of exhilaration.

The path twisted sharply, forcing the racers to weave through a dense cluster of trees. Capri spotted a gap between two towering pines and aimed for it, her snowmobile barely squeezing through. A branch scraped against her shoulder, but she didn't slow. Only yards away, the teenager from the starting line wasn't so lucky. His snowmobile caught a hidden root, sending him sprawling into the snow. She didn't look back.

The roar of engines reverberated through the mountains, mingling with the crunch of snow and the occasional shout from a racer. Capri's focus was razor-sharp, her senses heightened. She spotted a narrow ridge ahead, a treacherous section of the course that required absolute precision. The edge dropped off into a deep ravine, and one wrong move could spell disaster.

She gunned the throttle, her snowmobile screaming in protest as she sped across the ridge. Snow sprayed in her wake, the powdery mist catching the sunlight like shards of glass. Ahead, the scar-faced man was gaining ground. Capri gritted her teeth and pushed harder, her machine vibrating as it hit its top speed.

The next section of the course was a series of brutal jumps, each one designed to test the racers' skill and nerve. Capri approached the first jump, a natural ramp formed by a protruding rock. She leaned back slightly, lifting the snowmobile's nose as she launched into the air. For a split second, she was weightless, the world below her a blur. She landed hard, the impact jarring her bones but failing to slow her momentum.

The second jump came fast, followed by a sharp turn that forced her to lean precariously to one side. The snowmobile's treads bit into the ground, spraying a rooster tail of snow as she corrected her trajectory. Another racer tried to overtake her, but Capri veered sharply, cutting him off and forcing him to swerve into a bank of snow. She heard him curse loudly but didn't spare him a second thought.

The path grew even steeper, the incline testing the limits of the snowmobiles' engines. The sound of revving motors grew louder, echoing ominously off the surrounding peaks. Capri's arms ached from the effort of steering, but she welcomed the burn. She relished the challenge, the competition, the raw, untamed energy of the race.

Ahead, a particularly sharp turn forced her to brake hard. The snowmobile's treads skidded across the icy surface, and she felt the back end fishtail.

A curse escaped her lips as she adjusted her weight instinctively, righting the machine just in time to avoid a collision with a boulder. The near miss sent a fresh surge of adrenaline coursing through her.

Then she heard it—a deep, resonant rumble that wasn't coming from the engines. It was distant at first, almost imperceptible, but it grew louder with each passing second. Capri's stomach tightened as she realized what it was.

Instinct took over, and she slowed even further.

Like a distant growl of thunder, she heard it again—a low, deep rumble that didn't belong. Her stomach tightened as the sound grew louder, rolling through the mountains with a force that seemed to come from everywhere and nowhere.

The rumble wasn't just noise. She felt it in her bones, a vibration that passed through the snowmobile and into the ground beneath her. Fear coiled tight in her chest as she glanced up the mountainside. The pristine slope quivered, like a predator ready to pounce. Fractures spiderwebbed across the surface, and with a chilling inevitability, the first wave of snow began to slide.

"Avalanche!" she screamed, her voice lost in the roar. Her fellow racers were oblivious, their machines still roaring ahead. She gritted her teeth, veering off the track, her only thought to escape the deadly cascade before it consumed them all.

6

The roar started as a faint hum, low and deep like the earth clearing its throat. Reva froze mid-sentence, her hand gripping the edge of the truck bed. "What's that?" she whispered, though the looks on faces told her everyone else already knew.

"It's an avalanche," Charlie Grace said, her voice breaking. She shaded her eyes, squinting toward the distant slope where Capri had disappeared.

The girlfriends stood in a stunned line, the color draining from their faces as the mountain shifted before their eyes. A massive wall of snow tumbled down with terrifying force, swallowing the jagged rocks and sparse trees in its path.

"Oh my God," Lila gasped, her hand flying to her mouth. "They're right up there!"

Bodhi, standing near Capri's truck, frantically adjusted the knob on the helmet radio now strapped to his hip. His tan face paled as he pressed the button again and again. "Capri, do you copy? CAPRI! Come on, answer me!"

Static crackled back at him, cold and unforgiving.

"She has the blasted helmet on," Bodhi said, his voice rising with desperation. "Surely she can hear me!" He smacked the side of the radio, as though brute force could will Capri's voice to respond.

Nothing.

"We have to do something!" Charlie Grace snapped, gripping Reva's arm.

"What are we supposed to do?" Reva's calm veneer was cracking, her voice shaking as she scanned the horizon. "We're down here. They're—" She gestured helplessly toward the mountain, her throat tightening.

The sound of approaching footsteps cut through the panic. A small group of onlookers from the parking lot began to gather, murmuring in hushed tones as the spectacle unfolded. Nicola Cavendish, ever the town gossip, clutched her yappy Yorkie to her chest. "An avalanche?" she gasped, looking from the girlfriends to Bodhi. "Oh, Lord, are they trapped up there?"

Reva spun on her heel. "Nicola, that's a given. Either help or go home."

Nicola, affronted but obedient, stepped back with an indignant huff.

Lila grabbed Bodhi by the shoulders. "Try again. Try her again. Keep trying."

"I'm trying!" Bodhi shouted, his voice raw with frustration. "I don't even know if she—" He cut himself off, unwilling to say the words out loud. His hands trembled as he pressed the button again. "Capri, it's Bodhi. Please, tell me you're okay. Just... tell me something."

The static hissed and popped, cruel in its silence.

The girlfriends stood huddled together, eyes fixed on the mountain as the snow finally began to settle, leaving an eerie quiet in its wake. The once-pristine slope was now a jagged scar, the path of destruction painfully clear.

"They could've been anywhere," Lila said, trying to sound hopeful but failing miserably.

"Maybe they made it out of the way," Charlie Grace added, though tears rimmed her eyes.

"Yeah," Reva murmured, though her gaze didn't waver from the mountain. "Maybe."

Bodhi dropped the radio to his side, his shoulders slumping in defeat. "I'm going up there," he said, turning toward the transport vehicle.

"Bodhi, no," Lila said, grabbing his arm. "You don't even know where they are. You'll get yourself killed."

"I can't just stand here!" he shouted, pulling away. "I should've stopped her—I knew this would happen!"

Reva stepped forward, her voice frantic but firm. "Bodhi, listen to me. You're not going to help Capri by getting yourself caught in the aftermath. We need to wait for the rescue team."

As if on cue, the wail of a distant siren pierced the air. The girlfriends turned toward the sound, hope flickering in their eyes as a snow rescue vehicle crested the hill into the parking lot.

"Thank God," Charlie Grace breathed.

Bodhi didn't move, his hands curling into fists. "I should've done more," he whispered. "I should've—"

"You couldn't have stopped her," Lila said softly, placing a hand on his shoulder. "Capri does what she's going to do. You know that as well as we do."

The siren grew louder as the vehicle pulled in, its doors swinging open. A team of rescuers jumped out, gearing up for the climb. The girlfriends and Bodhi watched as the rescuers moved with efficiency, their calm demeanor a stark contrast to the panic rippling through the small group.

"We'll find her," one of them said, meeting Bodhi's frantic gaze. "We'll find all of them."

The words hung in the air, a fragile thread of hope as they turned back to the mountain.

The rumble of an engine cut through the voices shouting and equipment clattering as rescuers prepared for action. A cloud of dust and snow swirled in the air as Jake Carrington's pickup tore into the lot, skidding to a stop just feet from where the group had gathered. The door flew open, and Jake climbed out, his usual composed demeanor replaced with a frantic energy none of them had ever seen before. His rugged frame moved with purpose as he scanned the group and shoved gloves and a radio in his pocket. His gaze landed squarely on Bodhi.

"Is it true?" Jake's voice was rough, barely controlled. His eyes flicked to the distant mountain, then back to the others. "Is she up there?"

The silence that followed was answer enough.

Reva gave a small nod, her face pale and drawn.

Jake's jaw tightened, his breath coming out in quick, sharp bursts. He turned back to the mountain, his expression dark with determination.

Without another word, Jake strode toward a snowmobile parked near the edge of the lot. It belonged to the rescue team, but no one dared stop him. He swung a leg over the seat, his movements quick and decisive.

"Jake, wait!" Reva called out, stepping forward. "The rescue team is already—"

"They're too slow," he shot back, his voice hard, leaving no room for argument. His hands gripped the handlebars, his knuckles white. "I'm not waiting for them."

Before anyone could respond, Jake turned the key. The engine roared to life, the sound cutting through the frigid air. He twisted the throttle, and the snowmobile surged forward, spraying loose powder behind him. The girlfriends stood frozen, watching as he raced toward the treacherous slope, his figure growing smaller and smaller against the vast expanse of white.

"He's going to get himself killed," Lila whispered, her voice trembling.

Reva placed a hand on her shoulder, her eyes locked on Jake's retreating form. "He's not going to stop," she said quietly. "Not until he finds her."

The group stood in stunned silence; their breaths visible in the icy air as they watched him disappear into the snow-dusted wilderness.

Hope mingled with dread in her heart as Reva silently prayed he would find Capri—and make it back himself.

∼

CAPRI WOKE WITH A START, the icy bite of snow against her face snapping her into reality. For a moment, she couldn't move as her mind struggled to catch up to her body.

She grunted as she tried to shift. "What the—" She let her whisper fade as awareness—and fear—gripped her.

The...the avalanche.

She wasn't buried, but her limbs were weighed down by layers of snow, her arms partially pinned. Cold seeped through her clothes, sharp and unforgiving. She tried to shift and felt a jagged rock pressing into her back. The sharp discomfort jolted her, and then—white-hot pain shot through her legs.

She gasped, her breath puffing out in visible clouds. "No, no, no," she whispered, clenching her teeth as the pain spiraled out, radiating from her thighs. Her fingers moved shakily to brush away the snow around her legs. Her right foot was bent at an unnatural angle, her left pinned awkwardly against another rock.

A broken leg. Maybe two.

Panic crept in as her situation became horrifyingly clear. She was alone on a mountainside, swept off her snowmobile by the avalanche, and unable to move. Her breaths came faster, shallower, her chest tightening with every second. She tilted her head to look around, but all she could see was a vast sea of white and scattered debris—the remnants of her own reckless decision.

Even her helmet was missing, ripped off by the snow's force.

"Stupid," she muttered, her voice trembling as tears pricked at her eyes. "Why can't I just listen? Why do I always have to prove something?"

The memory of Bodhi's warning cut through her self-pity. He had told her to take the safer route. He'd practically begged her. But no, she had to charge ahead, had to prove she could master the most dangerous stretch. And now she was paying for it.

The ache in her legs grew more unbearable by the second, and with it, the icy grip of fear wrapped tighter around her. She might not be found right away. Depending on how far the snow slide had taken her down the mountain...maybe never.

She could have a compound fracture. She could be bleeding internally.

She might not survive.

The thought sent her spiraling, her mind racing through worst-case scenarios. She pictured herself succumbing to the cold, her friends, Jake, and her mother receiving the news of her body being recovered days, maybe weeks, later. The idea of them mourning her—of her mom burying another loved one—was almost more than she could bear.

"No," she said aloud, trying to steady herself. "Stop it. They'll find you. Someone will come."

But even as she said it, doubt gnawed at the edges of her mind. She had no idea how far she'd been swept, no clue if the rescuers would even know where to start. The snow covered everything.

The silence was deafening. She thought of the other racers, wondered if they were alive...or dead.

A sob broke free, and she clamped a hand over her mouth, fighting the rising tide of despair. Tears slid down her cheeks, hot against her frozen skin.

She couldn't fall apart now. Not yet. If she had any chance of surviving, she needed to stay calm, to think. But the reality of her helplessness pressed down harder than the snow around her.

She let her head fall back against the rock, staring up at the sky, an eerily clear expanse above her. Blue and cold and infinite.

"Great," she muttered bitterly. "Perfect day to die."

The thought chilled her more than the snow ever could. She didn't want to die. Not here. Not like this. But as the minutes dragged on and the pain in her legs grew sharper, Capri felt the icy tendrils of doubt tighten their grip. For once, she couldn't fix this herself. She could only hope someone else would.

The sound of her own ragged breathing was her only company as she lay there, waiting—praying—that help was on its way.

7

Jake Carrington squinted against the sun glaring off the snow, the cold air biting at his face even through the scarf wrapped around his neck. The snowmobile thrummed beneath him, a reliable hum that steadied his nerves as he maneuvered up the mountain. Every shift of the terrain under the snow—a slight give, a groan of pressure—sent his heart pounding. He was hyper-aware of the avalanche risk. Still, he pressed on, scanning the endless white expanse for any sign of Capri.

She'd ignored the warnings. That was Capri for you. Feisty, determined, a streak of stubbornness that had both exasperated and charmed him during the months they'd worked together to rebuild her mother's house. He'd admired her fire then, even when it was directed at him, but now it had gotten her into trouble. The thrill-seekers she'd followed up here were oblivious to the mountain's danger, and now she was missing. Jake's gut twisted. He had to find her. The thought of her buried under the snow was unbearable.

The snowmobile skidded as he crested a ridge. He eased off the throttle, scanning the area. His eyes caught movement—or what he thought was movement—near a cluster of rocks with pine branches sticking awkwardly out of the snow. Hope surged through him. He stopped the snowmobile, his boots crunching as he jumped off. Digging with his gloved hands, he clawed at the snow. But all he unearthed were shattered tree limbs.

"Damn it!" he muttered, his breath puffing in the icy air. He slammed his gloves against his thighs, his despair mounting.

Capri wasn't just any woman—she was becoming everything to him. He often caught himself watching her with quiet admiration. He often found himself studying her as she laughed with her friends, marveling at the way her smile lit up the entire room, like she carried her own sunshine. It wasn't just her beauty—though that alone could undo him—but the fierce determination she wore like armor and the vulnerability she tried so hard to hide beneath it.

The depth of his feelings startled him, tightening his chest at the mere thought of losing her.

He couldn't give up. He had to find her.

Climbing back onto the snowmobile, his hand hovered over the ignition switch. Then he heard it. A faint sound carried on the icy wind. He froze, straining to listen. Was it his imagination? He held his breath until it came again—a muffled noise, barely discernible. Could it be her?

Revving the snowmobile, he followed the sound to the edge of a pine tree grove, its branches broken like toothpicks. Among the littered landscape, fragments of a snowmobile glittered among the snow. His chest tightened as he spotted a helmet wedged in the branches of a tree.

Capri's helmet.

Relief and fear surged in equal measure as he abandoned his snowmobile and sprinted toward the tree, his boots sinking deep into the snow.

"Capri!" he shouted, his voice cracking. He didn't even

realize tears were streaming down his face until he wiped his cheek and felt the wetness.

Silence answered him at first. Then, faint and weak, her voice drifted from the other side of the rock cropping. "Jake?"

His heart leapt. "Capri! I'm coming!" He scrambled over the rock, slipping on the ice but refusing to slow down. When he rounded the corner, he spotted her, half-buried in the snow but alive. Her face was pale, a scrape visible on her cheek, but her eyes were open and locked on him.

"Jake," she murmured, tears pooling in her eyes. "You found me."

He dropped to his knees beside her, brushing the snow off her jacket. "Of course I found you. You scared the hell out of me, Capri." He quickly scanned her torso, concern mapping his expression.

A weak laugh escaped her lips. "I thought I'd...never see you again."

"Don't say that," he said, his voice thick. "Don't you ever say that."

Her fingers trembled as she reached for his hand. "I...I was so stupid. I didn't listen."

"Yeah, you were," he said, his lips twitching into a faint smile despite the situation. "But that's you. Always pushing boundaries. And you know what? It's one of the things I love about you."

Her eyes widened. "Love?"

He cupped her face gently, his thumb brushing the scrape on her cheek. "Yeah, Capri. I love you. And I'll say it a hundred more times once we get you out of here."

Tears spilled from her eyes as she whispered, "I love you, too."

The admission filled him with a warmth that cut through the cold. He kissed her forehead, lingering for a moment before pulling back. "We're going to get you out of here. Are you hurt anywhere?"

"My leg," she admitted, wincing as she shifted slightly. "It's pinned."

"Okay," he said, his voice steady. He pulled the radio from his parka jacket. "I've found her, Bodhi," he said, his voice firm despite the tears still streaming down his face. "I need backup. She's alive but injured. We're near the rock cropping on the south ridge."

"Copy that," came the response. "Hang tight. Help is on the way."

Jake put the radio down and squeezed Capri's hand. "Help is coming. You just hold on for me, okay?"

She nodded weakly. "I'll hold on, Jake. I promise."

Ten minutes later, a helicopter hovered above, its blades slicing through the icy mountain air with a deafening roar that drowned out the frantic calls of the rescue team inside. Snow whipped around them in a blinding frenzy, stinging Jake's face and mixing with the sharp scent of pine and exhaust. He stood at the edge of the slope, his heart pounding as he watched the rescue basket lower toward Capri. She lay still, her face pale against the stark white snow, her leg bent at an unnatural angle.

"Eight of the nine missing have been located," a rescue worker shouted over the din, his voice barely cutting through the thunder of the rotors. Jake nodded, a flicker of relief mixed with the gnawing dread that refused to release its grip. He was thankful, but Capri's condition still consumed him.

As the basket rose, swaying precariously in the gusts, Jake reached up to steady it, his hands trembling against the metal. He followed the team who were now on the ground to his abandoned snowmobile, then turned to wave down the group now cresting the ridge. His hand signaled he was leaving the vehicle behind, but his mind remained on Capri.

Jake climbed aboard the helicopter, the vibrations coursing through him as the door slammed shut. He reached for her hand, cold and limp in his own, and gripped it tightly as if sheer willpower could hold her together. The sound of the rotors filled the cramped cabin, and the faint, sterile smell of the medical supplies was a stark contrast to the wilderness they were leaving behind.

The rescuers moved swiftly, their voices clipped and efficient as they worked to stabilize Capri in the narrow cabin. An oxygen mask was secured over her face, and a medic adjusted the straps on the splint that now encased her broken leg. Jake shifted out of the way as they worked, his heart hammering with every grim exchange of words between the team.

The helicopter's rotors thundered in his ears as the aircraft lifted from the ground. When one of the medics paused to check equipment, Jake bent forward, brushing a tender kiss against her forehead. The warmth of her skin, though faint, sent a surge of determination through him.

"I'm here," he murmured, his voice low but firm. "And I'm not leaving your side. Not now, not ever."

"I'm sorry," she whispered. "I—"

"Shh. Everything's going to be okay," he promised.

As the helicopter tilted and banked in the direction of Jackson and the hospital, Jake tightened his grip on her hand. The chaos around him faded, leaving only the resolute promise that he would see her through this—no matter what.

8

St. John's Health in Jackson was a little over an hour from the race site, but for Charlie Grace, the drive felt like a lifetime. The temperatures had dropped in the past couple of hours and now the roads were slick in spots, making the trip even slower. She gripped the wheel of her old ranch truck, her knuckles white, and replayed the afternoon's events in her mind.

An avalanche. Capri. Buried.

"Faster, Charlie Grace," Reva urged, her voice tight with worry.

"I'm going as fast as I can. This isn't a new truck you know," Charlie Grace snapped, immediately wincing at her own sharp tone. "Sorry, nerves."

Beside them, Lila was furiously tapping on her phone screen.

"Who are you texting now?" Reva asked, glancing over with a frown.

"Camille," Lila replied without looking up. "I need to let her know I won't be home tonight so she won't worry."

Reva's brows shot up. "Camille's in Thunder Mountain? Isn't she supposed to be at school?"

Lila's thumb paused mid-text, knowing her secret was now out. Her expression turned guarded. "That's...complicated. Let's just say it's a story for another day."

Charlie Grace glanced at Lila, curiosity tugging at her. She opened her mouth to press for details but caught herself. Now wasn't the time. She jammed her foot on the accelerator and refocused on the road ahead. Capri needed them. Everything else could wait.

The rest of the long, winding drive down the mountain passed in tense silence, the weight of their worry pressing down on them like the low-hanging clouds outside. Charlie Grace anchored her hands on the steering wheel so tightly her knuckles ached, her thoughts racing between the slippery mountain roads and the unknown waiting for them at the hospital.

Reva stared out the window, her hands twisting in her lap, while Lila occasionally glanced at her phone as if willing it to light up with good news. The closer they got to Jackson, the heavier the air in the car seemed to grow.

When the glowing sign for St. John's Health finally came into view, Charlie Grace let out a breath she hadn't realized she was holding. "Almost there," she said quietly, more to herself than anyone else.

Reva straightened, her eyes fixed on the hospital entrance as they pulled into the lot. She pointed. "Hurry."

Charlie Grace parked as close as she could, barely waiting for the truck to come to a full stop before she opened the door and followed the others to the entrance.

Charlie Grace's foot tapped impatiently as she waited for the glass entry doors to slide open. When they finally did, she had to sidestep around an elderly man in a wheelchair and the curt nurse pushing him through the front doors. Charlie Grace mumbled, "Excuse me," and darted inside, close on the heels of her friends.

The main lobby of St. John's was functional and unassuming, designed for efficiency rather than comfort. The pale beige walls were interrupted by large directories and informational posters about health services, and the faint scent of antiseptic hung in the air. A central reception desk, with its rounded counter and cluttered computer stations, was the hub of activity as staff members directed visitors and answered phones.

Reva hurried forward, stopping in front of a woman with a round face and deep dimples. "Capri Jacobs. They brought her here by helicopter?"

The woman took her sweet time looking up from her computer screen. "I'm sorry. Who are you looking for?"

"There was an avalanche," Lila nearly shouted. "They brought her here."

Recognition dawned. "Oh my, yes. I heard about that." She pointed down a corridor. "The emergency department is down there. Turn left at the end of the hallway."

"Thanks," Charlie Grace said, then broke into a sprint, making her way in that direction. Reva and Lila followed close behind.

The emergency waiting room was already packed. Word of the accident had moved faster than a train and dozens of familiar faces from Thunder Mountain had already gathered, murmuring in clusters or sitting tensely in chairs. The town had turned out for Capri—Nicola Cavendish sat with Sweetpea in her lap, whispering in hushed tones to her husband, Wooster. Typically, dogs were not allowed in the hospital, but Wooster's bank had provided the money needed for an expansion of the pediatrics wing and concessions were made.

Pastor Pete stood with Annie near the coffee station; their

heads bowed in prayer. Albie Barton, the town reporter, paced the room, notebook in hand and a pencil behind his ear.

Oma Griffith sat in one of the stiff, gray vinyl chairs between Betty Dunning and Dorothy Vaughn, clutching their hands. The older women looked pale; their eyes swollen as though they'd been crying. Bodhi was slumped against the wall by the vending machines, his usually carefree expression replaced with one of raw guilt.

Charlie Grace scanned the room, spotting Jake pacing near the wall mounted with a television.

Reva saw him as well and made a beeline in that direction. "Any news?"

Nicola Cavendish turned sharply from where she sat, her phone in her hand. Without waiting for Jake to respond, she stood and offered a report. "She's stable. They've taken her for scans to check the extent of her injuries." Her voice was steady, but her red-rimmed eyes betrayed her emotions.

Charlie Grace's ex-husband arrived, his hair disheveled and his shirt buttoned wrong. "What happened?" Gibbs' voice was tight, almost accusing, as he looked at Bodhi.

Bodhi's head snapped up, his eyes glistening. "Jake found her on the north slope, next to the scarp face of the mountain." His voice cracked. "I warned her not to take that route."

Charlie Grace nodded, swallowing hard. "Where is she now?"

"Like Nicola said, they took her to imaging," Annie answered. "The nurse said they'd update us as soon as they know anything."

Nicola quickly added, "I hope she has no head injuries. I heard the helmet was ripped right off her head in the force of the snow."

"Capri Jacob is tougher than anyone I know," Pastor Pete said quietly, his calm voice interrupting the tension. "And God has got this."

Reva nodded, wiping her eyes. "She'll pull through. She has to."

Hours passed with agonizing slowness. Charlie Grace alternated between standing, pacing, and leaning against the wall, arms crossed. A nurse appeared every so often, calling names, but none of the updates were for Capri.

"She'll be okay," Lila said, her tone more hopeful than certain.

Jake didn't respond. Instead, he stared at the doors leading to where they had wheeled Capri earlier, looking helpless.

The waiting room remained a hive of activity. People came and went, their concern for Capri evident in the whispered conversations and worried glances. Nicola approached, offering Reva a cup of coffee, while Pastor Pete gathered a small group to pray.

The television mounted on the wall blared softly, drawing the attention of everyone seated. A local news reporter stood bundled in a thick down jacket, her breath visible in the frigid air as she spoke into the microphone. Behind her, the Tetons loomed, their peaks blanketed with snow.

"*This is Kelly Morgan reporting live from the base of the Devil's Staircase in the Teton Range, where an avalanche earlier today triggered a dramatic rescue effort,*" she began, her voice steady despite the obvious chill in the air.

"*Authorities were alerted around noon after spectators gathered to watch a snowmobile race on the north slope witnessed the snow give way, triggering a massive avalanche that barreled down into the steep chutes below. Several racers were caught in the slide, tragically buried beneath tons of snow.*"

The camera cut to footage of rescue workers in bright orange jackets, some probing the snow with poles, others shouting commands over the howling wind.

"*Search and rescue teams responded immediately, deploying helicopters, ground crews, and avalanche dogs to comb the area. Despite* their heroic efforts, only one racer was found alive—a local resident and business owner. She was pulled from the snow suffering from hypothermia and multiple injuries.

"Tragically, other racers caught in the avalanche did not survive. Officials have not yet released their names, pending notification of their families. This devastating event underscores the dangerous conditions in the backcountry."

The screen transitioned to a wide shot of the snow-covered slope, the sunlight glinting off the pristine yet treacherous surface.

"The area, known as Devil's Staircase, is infamous for its extreme terrain and unpredictable conditions. Despite precautions taken prior to the race, including blasts to bring down unstable snow, experts say recent heavy winter snowfall, combined with rising temperatures and weak spring snowpack, created the ideal conditions for an avalanche."

The reporter's expression turned serious as she addressed the camera directly. "*Officials are urging residents and visitors to avoid backcountry areas like this until conditions stabilize. The danger level remains high, and with more snow in the forecast, the risk of additional slides is significant.*"

The feed remained fixed on Kelly, the wind tugging at her hood. "*We'll continue to monitor this story and provide updates on the condition of the rescued individual, who has been transported to St. John's Health in Jackson for treatment. Reporting live from Devil's Staircase, I'm Kelly Morgan for KJAX News.*"

The screen cut back to the anchor desk, but the waiting room remained silent, the weight of the report hanging in the air.

∽

JAKE STAYED ROOTED IN PLACE, his thoughts consumed by Capri —her fiery determination, her quick wit, the way her eyes sparkled when she argued with him. The idea of losing her was unbearable.

He replayed the rescue in his mind like a bad dream he couldn't wake up from. The deafening emergency engine sirens, the frantic calls of the search teams, and the endless minutes of him combing through the snow-laden landscape, searching for any sign of Capri—it all felt like a lifetime compressed into a few horrifying hours.

He remembered the sickening dread that gripped him when someone shouted they'd found a body, only to realize it wasn't moving. And then came the moment when he veered onto the unmarked path along the scarp face. His hunch told him Capri would not follow a tidy, marked trail.

He spotted the pieces of snowmobile and then heard her voice. Frantically, he got to her and pulled Capri out, pale and broken but alive. His chest had constricted so tightly that he thought he might pass out right there. She had trouble talking, her lips tinged blue from the cold. Seeing her like that—so small, so vulnerable—made him realize how deeply she'd embedded herself into his life. She wasn't just the fiery woman who challenged him at every turn. She had become his anchor, his reason for wanting more than just his quiet, solitary existence.

The thought of losing her had terrified him in a way nothing else ever had, and now, standing in the hospital, the fear still clung to him, raw and unrelenting.

Minutes dragged into hours while he and the others sat in those hospital chairs, drinking stale coffee and hoping for news. The wait was interrupted by a stern voice coming over the PA. "Paging pediatrics. Paging pediatrics."

A woman with a stethoscope draped around her neck entered from behind two automated doors at the end of the hallway. As she saw the waiting friends and their worried faces, her expression turned sympathetic.

Reva popped up from her seat. "Do you have news on Capri Jacobs?"

"It looks like your friend suffered no life-threatening internal injuries. Beyond a bruised spleen, she's remarkably unscathed." She paused letting the information sink in. "She did sustain compound fractures to her right femoral shaft and ankle. As earlier suspected, these injuries are going to require surgery. They are prepping her now."

Lila's hand went to her throat. "Can we see her?"

The nurse shook her head. "I'm afraid not. She's been heavily sedated to relieve the pain. We'll be wheeling her into the operating room very shortly." She held up a clip board. "Now, I'll need a main contact person from her immediate family. That would be—?"

Several in the room glanced at one another. While Capri's mother had been notified, she wouldn't be arriving for hours.

Reva stepped forward. "I'll be the contact." She pulled the pen from the nurse's fingers and filled out her name and cell number. When finished, she handed the clipboard and pen back. "We'll all be right here, though. None of us are leaving until Capri is out of surgery and okay." She looked around for confirmation and was met with enthusiastic nods.

Jake stepped by Reva's side and placed his hand on her shoulder before turning to the nurse. "Please alert us as soon as you know anything."

Reva dug in her purse and handed the woman her business card. "I'm the mayor of Thunder Mountain," she said, pointing.

The nurse smiled. "Of course. We'll add your information to our system so you can call back and see how the surgery is going."

"Perfect. How long do you expect the surgery to take?"

"Several hours," the nurse reported. She scanned the group. "I'd suggest you all might go get something to eat. We have a cafeteria. The food isn't restaurant quality, but it's good."

Jake shook his head. "Thank you, but no. I'm not leaving."

The nurse hugged the clipboard to her chest and offered a commiserative smile. "We're good at what we do. Our surgeons are top-notch."

Jake nodded. "Still, I want to be here. Close."

Charlie Grace, Lila, and Reva followed suit. "We're staying, too."

Pastor Pete patted Annie's back as she laid her head on his shoulder. "I suppose we should go get everyone some food," she suggested. She motioned to the Knit Wit ladies. "Oma, Dorothy? Why don't you come down with us and get a bite?"

Slowly, most of those who were gathered followed Pastor Pete and Annie down a long hall leading to the cafeteria. Except for Bodhi. He elected to stay.

The wait began again. This time in earnest. The hands on the wall clock seemed to inch forward at the speed of a slow creeping lava flow.

"Call them, Reva," Charlie Grace urged. "It's been a couple of hours, and the nurse said it was okay for you to check in occasionally."

Just as Reva was lifting her phone, it buzzed. Jake stretched over Capri's friend's shoulder to see—unknown caller. Moments ticked by as he listened to the one-sided conversation.

When Reva finally hung up, Jake was about to explode. "What did they say?"

Reva's voice was shaky but calm. "They're repairing some of the damage now—concentrating on the femoral injury. She's doing well. The nurse said she'd call with another update when she can."

Jake thanked her, then buried his attention in his phone where he researched orthopedic techniques and recovery times for Capri's injuries. Like always, there seemed to be conflicting information. One respected medical site said healing time could extend into months, with even more months of rehab.

Capri would not like that. Being laid up and unable to do what she loved would be hard to take. Then there was the fact she couldn't live on her own without some sort of help, at least in the near interim.

Reva seemed to have come to the same conclusion. "You know, Capri is not going to be able to remain alone at her house. She'll have to move in with one of us."

"I'll move in with her," Jake stated plainly as he gathered empty Styrofoam cups. "I'll take care of her." His tone left no room for discussion.

"I have a feeling she's going to be in the hospital for a good while," Lila offered. "I broke my wrist playing soccer in high school. It took forever to heal. Capri's injuries are much more extensive. That leg break may require traction."

A noise from down the hall caught their attention.

In all the commotion, they nearly missed seeing a man with graying hair at the temples enter the waiting room wearing blue scrubs. He was followed by two women, one with a clipboard and deep-set eyes that scanned the room, taking inventory of those seated and waiting for information.

He cleared his throat. "Excuse me. I'm Dr. McCord, Capri's surgeon."

Their talking immediately ceased. Jake and Reva simultaneously moved for him. "Doctor?" Reva said, her voice revealing how grueling the wait had been for her.

"Let's everybody take a seat."

The doctor pulled his surgical cap from his head. "First, Capri is out of danger. At least for now. Femoral breaks like this can be gnarly and cause havoc with the circulatory system. So, it's always important that these situations be remedied as quickly as possible."

Relief swept through the group like a wave. Reva covered

her face with her hands, shoulders shaking. Charlie Grace hugged Lila tightly. Bodhi let out a breath he seemed to have been holding for hours.

"And the surgery?" Jake ventured.

"This surgery was fairly arduous and will be one of several before we're through. We've placed an intramedullary rod to stabilize the femoral break and did what we could to repair the structural damage to her knees. She had a torn meniscus and damaged ligaments. The ankle repair will happen tomorrow. We don't like having patients anesthetized for long periods of time when we can help it." He drew a deep breath. "Capri is young. She's strong and otherwise healthy. While the road to full recovery will be a challenge and will take time, I have every reason to believe this young lady will get through this and will eventually be walking like normal, barring complications."

"How much time?" Lila asked, voicing the question running through everyone's mind.

"That can depend on a number of factors. But likely we're talking months," the doctor told them.

Reva reached for Jake. "Can we see her?"

"She's being moved to recovery now," the doctor told them. "She'll be groggy but stable. I'll have a nurse come get you once she's settled."

"Thank you, Doc," Jake said, his voice gruff with emotion.

The surgeon nodded. "She's tough. That helped her a lot today."

In that brief moment, emotion rolled over Jake like ocean waves pounding the shoreline.

He couldn't help himself. In relief, he flung his arms around the doctor's broad shoulders. "Thank you for taking care of my girl. You don't know—" He let his voice fade.

Dr. McCord gently patted his back. "I do know."

Minutes later, a nurse appeared on the scene and offered to take them to see Capri.

"You coming?" Reva asked, pulling at his arm.

"C'mon," Lila demanded. "Let's go see her."

Jake followed Capri's friends down a hall and through a large circular area. In the center was a nurses' station with bleeping monitors mounted on the counter. Beyond were individual areas cordoned off by glass walls. Those with patients were dimly lit. Some were darkened and had empty beds, neatly made up for the next people unfortunate enough to need them.

Finally, they came to a stop.

Beyond the glass, Capri was positioned in a bed. Her leg was suspended midair with a steel bar and chains. The ankle was wrapped with ice packs. Machines with blinking lights stood sentinel on either side of the hospital bed and an IV dripline was attached to one of her hands.

Her face was pale, but the rise and fall of her chest was steady.

Reva was the first to approach, brushing a strand of hair from Capri's face. "Oh, honey," she whispered, tears slipping down her cheeks.

Charlie Grace stood on the other side of the bed, her hand on Capri's arm. "You scared us, Cap. But you're okay now."

Lila nodded. "We're here for you, Capri. All of us."

Jake finally stepped into the room, his boots thudding softly against the floor. He moved to the foot of the bed, his gaze fixed on Capri. She stirred slightly, her eyes fluttering open.

"Hey," he said softly, leaning closer. "You gave us all a scare."

Capri's lips curved into a faint smile. "Sorry...didn't mean to." Her voice was barely a whisper before her eyes drifted shut again.

Jake swallowed hard, his throat tight. He reached out, brushing his fingers lightly against her hand. "Rest up, Trouble. We've got you now."

Jake's chest tightened. But not in a bad way. In that moment, he was more than grateful. Capri had suffered an accident that had left them all reeling. In the end, she was going to be all right. The recovery would, no doubt, be long and arduous. While difficult, Capri would do the required work and regain her physical abilities in full.

But until then, he wasn't planning to leave her side.

9

It was nearly dawn when Charlie Grace dropped off Lila at her house. "Hope you get some sleep. It's been a long day...and night." Charlie Grace brushed a kiss on Lila's cheek, and they briefly hugged.

Lila reached for the door handle of the old truck, feeling it wiggle loosely under her grip before it finally gave way. "You, too. And thanks for the ride." She got out, waved, and shut the passenger door.

The frosty air of the mountain morning bit softly against her skin, carrying the crisp, clean scent of pine. The faint outline of the moon hung low in the predawn sky, its pale light casting a silvery glow that lit the winding path to her porch, making the landscape seem both ethereal and still, as if holding its breath for what lay ahead.

She savored the sight and sighed. Sometimes it felt like she was losing the moon.

Lila stepped into her warm kitchen, the familiar hum of the refrigerator and the faint smell of vanilla from the diffuser grounding her after the long, emotional day. Even at this early hour, Camille sat at the table wearing a bathrobe, her hands wrapped around a steaming mug of tea, her face anxious.

"How's Capri?" Camille asked before Lila could take off her coat. The question carried a tremor of worry, and Lila paused to meet her daughter's eyes.

"She'll be okay," Lila said, her voice calm but tinged with weariness. She hung her coat on the hook by the door and sat across from Camille. "Her leg's badly broken, and she needed surgery, but thankfully, there's no spinal injury or head trauma. Jake is moving in with her to take care of everything while she recovers. It's going to be a long road, but Capri's tough."

Camille nodded, her shoulders relaxing a little, but her lips remained pressed into a thin line. No doubt her daughter had been worried. She'd always admired Capri, the fearless friend of her mother who seemed unshakable even in the most chaotic of times.

"That's good," Camille said softly. "Jake seems like a great guy. He'll take good care of her."

"He will," Lila replied with certainty. She reached for Camille's hand, her fingers brushing over the younger woman's knuckles. "But let's talk about you. Have you given any more thought to your plans? When you'll return to school?"

Camille's expression stiffened instantly, and she leaned back, cradling the mug against her chest as though it were a shield.

"I've made my decision," she said, her tone defensive. "I'm going to take classes remotely."

"Remote classes?" Lila repeated, her brows knitting. Despite her earlier reservations, after careful consideration, Lila now firmly believed the less disruption to Camille's education, the better. "Camille, I understand that's an option, but is it really the best one? You've always dreamed of the college experience. Living on campus, making friends, being part of something bigger. You can still do that. There are so many girls who go to class pregnant, who find a way to make it work."

"Not me," Camille said sharply. "I've already enrolled for online classes. It's done."

Lila's stomach twisted. She forced herself to take a calming breath before speaking again. "But why? Camille, you've been so excited about college since you were little. Why throw that away?" Let alone how hard Lila had worked to get her there, she thought.

"I'm not throwing anything away," Camille snapped, her eyes flashing. "This is what's best for me now. Isn't that what you always taught me? To figure out what works and stick to it?"

Lila hesitated, searching her daughter's face for some crack in the armor, some sign that this wasn't just stubborn defiance but fear or hurt she could soothe. But Camille's jaw was set, her gaze unyielding. Whatever was driving her refusal to return to campus, she wasn't ready to share it.

"I just want you to think about your future," Lila said quietly. "About what this decision might mean for the path you're on." She paused. "Everything you do now will affect what's ahead for not only you...but your baby." She swallowed, still finding it hard to push those foreign words from her lips.

Camille's shoulders stiffened, and she stared down into her tea. "I am thinking about my future," she said, her voice barely above a whisper. "I'm doing what I need to do, just like you did when you got your degree online. You worked, raised me, and made it happen. Why can't I?"

Lila's chest tightened. It wasn't the same, not to her. She'd sacrificed the traditional college experience for necessity, for survival. She'd wanted more for Camille, had dreamed of her daughter walking across a campus brimming with possibility, surrounded by friends and a world of new opportunities. But this pregnancy had rerouted Camille's life, pushing her down a path that Lila hadn't imagined for her.

"I'm proud of you," Lila said finally, her voice steady but soft. "No matter what. You know that, right?"

Camille nodded, but she didn't look up. The silence between them stretched, filled with the weight of things unspoken. Lila wanted to press, to understand, but something in her daughter's posture told her it was better to wait. For now, this was all Camille could give.

As Lila rose to start tidying up the kitchen, her gaze lingered on the faint reflection of mother and daughter in the window over the sink. Two women standing at different crossroads, bound together by love and the hope that the choices they made today would lead to brighter tomorrows. And like the moon, waxing and waning in its quiet rhythm, they would find their way, even in the shadowed moments.

For every phase had its purpose, and every path its light.

10

Charlie Grace Rivers turned her truck into the gravel driveway of the Teton Trails Guest Ranch, the crunch of tires on ice the only sound in the quiet predawn morning. Her sharp eyes immediately caught sight of a familiar truck parked near the barn. Gibbs' truck.

A flicker of curiosity mixed with annoyance tightened her chest. What was he doing here? Normally, Gibbs didn't show up for work on time, let alone hours early.

With a resigned sigh, she parked her truck near the porch and stepped out, taking care not to slip. Her gaze lingered on the barn, where faint cracks of light peeked through the edges of the big sliding door.

Charlie Grace adjusted her hat, tugged her coat tighter against the crisp chill, and made her way in that direction. The scent of hay and wood smoke hung in the air, and the mountains stood sentinel in the distance, their snowy peaks a silent witness to whatever awaited her.

Charlie Grace's marriage to Gibbs had been a masterclass in frustration. He was unreliable and untrustworthy, with a wandering eye and a tendency to let his charm roam as freely as a stray calf. That was bad enough, but he was also irresponsibly absent when it came to the heavy lifting. The ranch work, the housework, raising their daughter, Jewel—it all fell squarely on Charlie Grace's shoulders. Gibbs, meanwhile, played the fun parent, swooping in for movie nights and ice cream runs, leaving her to nag about homework and clean up the messes he left behind.

She'd about throttled her dad when he went behind her back and hired Gibbs to help at the ranch. It was no surprise when she caught Gibbs in the hayloft with Albie's niece, Lizzy —or when he got her pregnant.

Since marrying Lizzy, Gibbs seemed—for lack of a better word—different. His womanizing days appeared to have settled, replaced by the steady responsibilities of being a husband and, more recently, a father.

Maybe he believed this was his chance. A fresh start. A do-over. Maybe he'd finally decided to be the man he'd always claimed he could be. Charlie Grace couldn't decide whether that notion annoyed her or made her hopeful—for Lizzy and the baby's sake, of course. Not for her own.

She reached the barn and hesitated for a moment, hand poised on the door handle. The faint sound of muffled voices reached her ears. Her brow furrowed as she slid the door open just enough to slip inside, her boots barely making a sound on the barn's dirt floor.

Inside, Gibbs stood near the tack wall, his broad back to her, gesturing animatedly as he spoke to someone out of view. The warm light from the overhead bulb cast long shadows across the hay-strewn floor, and the scene felt oddly intimate, even though Charlie Grace doubted it was anything more than practical ranch talk.

"Gibbs," she called, her voice cutting through the barn's quiet. Her tone was calm, but it carried the weight of years of shared history—some good, some not.

Gibbs turned, his expression startled before quickly settling into that familiar, boyish grin. "Charlie Grace. Didn't expect to see you here."

Charlie Grace glanced around. "Who were you talking to?"

"Who? Me?"

She frowned. "No, the scarecrow in the corner. Of course, you." She looked around again, puzzled. "Are you alone?"

Gibbs' face flamed as he turned and patted the nuzzle on the horse in the pen. "Just chatting with Mr. Ed."

"You were carrying on a conversation with a horse?" She shook her head. "Whatever."

He dipped his hand in a bucket of grain and brought it to the horse's mouth. "Hey, we're buddies, aren't we Mr. Ed?"

He turned. "How's Capri doing?"

Charlie Grace slipped her hands deep inside her coat pockets. "No doubt, she'll be in traction for a couple of weeks. Then, when she's released and comes home, she'll still need a lot of assistance. Jake's stepping up to take care of her while she recovers."

"What about her mother?"

She shrugged. "Her mom is pretty wrapped up in her new husband. I don't think she wanted to leave him in Idaho, even temporarily." While she didn't say so, it irked her that Capri's mother was so self-focused. Especially after everything Capri had always done to take care of her mom.

She supposed it was true. There were women whose sole being and purpose was wrapped up in a man at the expense of everything, and everyone, else.

Charlie Grace let out a heavy sigh. "I doubt Capri will be riding any snowmobiles or charging rapids in a raft any time soon. She'll be doing well to get herself dressed every day."

Gibbs nodded, his smile fading as concern crept into his eyes. "That's tough. She's lucky it wasn't worse."

Charlie Grace nodded, the memory still raw. "Yeah. When I

saw the snowface start to slide, my heart dropped. It's terrifying how fast something like that can happen, how small you feel in the face of it." Her voice wavered slightly, and she pressed her lips together to steady herself. "For a moment, I thought we would for sure lose her."

Gibbs stepped closer, his usual swagger replaced with an unexpected gentleness. "Hey, it's okay. You did everything you could, and Capri's tough. She'll get through this." He placed his hand on the sleeve of her coat and squeezed.

The sincerity in his voice surprised her. They were talking like friends again, sharing a moment that felt real and unguarded. For a brief second, she thought maybe this was what they'd lost somewhere along the way.

And then, as if on cue, Gibbs shattered the moment.

"Speaking of getting through," he began, scratching the back of his neck, "I was wondering if I could get an advance on my paycheck. I'm running a little low right now."

Charlie Grace's brows shot up. "An advance? Gibbs, we've talked about budgeting before. What happened?"

He hesitated, shifting his weight. "Well, Brewster Findley was selling his spotting scope. I picked it up for only two hundred bucks. That's half of what it sells for new. If I didn't scoop it up, someone else would have."

"A spotting scope?" Charlie Grace's voice was flat, the disbelief clear.

"Yeah," Gibbs said earnestly, as though this explanation would smooth everything over. "It'll be great for hunting season. You can't pass up a deal like that."

Charlie Grace stared at him, torn between exasperation and the tiniest flicker of amusement.

Same old Gibbs.

"Truth is, Gibbs. Cash flow is tight for the ranch right now. I really can't advance you the money."

"You know I'm good for it," he argued.

"That's not the issue. My statement is one hundred percent accurate. There's no money to spare in the ranch's bank accounts. Not until tourist season arrives."

Gibbs hesitated. "What about you personally? Can you spare a couple of hundred so I make rent? My landlord is cracking down on late payments, and I'd rather not end up living out of my truck. That might not sit well with Lizzy and the baby. I'll pay you back as soon as I can, Charlie Grace. You know I always do."

Charlie Grace folded her arms and studied him. Same pleading tone, same excuse, same tired promises. Gibbs Nichols might as well be a broken record, spinning the same sorry song he'd been singing for years.

"Gibbs, you've got to stop coming to me like this. You're a grown man," she said, her voice firm but not unkind. "I can't keep bailing you out every time you hit a rough patch. You've got to figure out how to stand on your own two feet."

His face tightened, and for a moment, she thought he might argue. But then, like always, he softened into the charming grin that had once worked so well on her.

"Come on, Charlie Grace. Don't be like that. You know I'd do the same for you."

She let out a soft laugh, shaking her head. "No, Gibbs. You wouldn't. That's the thing about you—you're always looking for someone to fix things for you, to catch you when you fall."

He opened his mouth, then closed it again, as if searching for the right response but coming up empty.

"I'm sorry," she said, gentler now. "I really am. But this time, you're going to have to figure it out on your own."

For a moment, Gibbs just stared at her, his grin slipping into something harder to read. Then he shrugged, shoved his hands into his pockets, and muttered, "Guess I'll figure something out, then."

As he turned and walked away, Charlie Grace felt a pang of

sadness. There was a time she might have handed him the money without a second thought, believing she was helping him, believing he might change. But she'd grown to know better.

Gibbs Nichols was a master at landing on his feet—and that would never change.

She watched him head outside and toward the feeding bins, his boots kicking up powdery snow. She stood gazing at his retreat for several seconds before turning and heading for the house.

On the way, she looked up at the fading moon and murmured to herself, "The trouble with Gibbs isn't that he's stuck in a rut. It's that he's made the rut his home."

11

Reva pulled into the parking lot of Moose Chapel just as the sun dipped below the horizon, casting long, amber shadows across the gravel. Her hands tightened on the steering wheel as she drew a deep breath. The chapel's familiar log frame loomed ahead, its cross silhouetted against a lavender sky. The sight had always brought her comfort, but tonight, it felt like a lifeline.

Inside, the faint scent of coffee mingled with the aged wood of the tiny sanctuary. She nodded to a few familiar faces in the hallway before making her way down the narrow staircase to the basement, the soft hum of muted conversations and the clinking of coffee cups growing louder with each step.

The room was simple—folding chairs arranged in a circle, a table against the wall holding a coffee urn and a stack of cookies on a paper plate. But to Reva, this was sacred ground. This place had seen her at her worst, and, over the years, at her best. Tonight, though, she felt like she was back at the starting line.

The familiar creak of the old wooden floor announced

Reva's arrival as she stepped into the room. A few heads turned, and friendly smiles greeted her. "Evening, Reva," said Jim, a wiry man in his sixties who always arrived early to set up the chairs. He lifted his coffee cup in a small salute.

"Evening, Jim," Reva replied, offering him a tired smile as she hung her coat on the hook by the door. "How's that grandbaby of yours?"

"Keeping us on our toes," he said with a chuckle. "You'd think I'd forgotten how much energy toddlers have."

"You probably did," called out Dot Montgomery from the coffee table, her bangles clinking as she poured herself a cup. "But they're good for keeping you young."

Reva nodded in agreement as she moved toward her usual seat. "Lord knows Lucan has enough energy for three toddlers. I could use some of that stamina," she said, settling into the chair and taking a deep breath. "Feels like it's been a week and a half since Monday."

A few chuckles rippled through the group, and the warm, familiar hum of conversation continued as more people filtered into the room.

Reva glanced around the circle, the familiar faces of the group giving her a sense of solace. She was not alone here, but the ache in her chest felt isolating. She hadn't felt this fragile in years—not since the early days, when the pull of alcohol felt like an unstoppable tide.

She folded her hands tightly in her lap. Her pulse raced as she replayed the scene of Capri's accident in her mind—the sharp edge of panic in her friends' voices as sirens approached. The memory refused to leave her, swirling with the guilt she couldn't shake.

She knew how dangerous that mountain could be. She should have done more to stop Capri from taking such a reckless risk. As mayor of Thunder Mountain, she might have even used her official capacity to pull rank and convince the organizers to shut down the race. Lives would not have been lost. Capri would not be laid up in a hospital bed in traction.

When the time came, Reva stood. Her chair creaked softly as she pushed it back, and the room fell quiet. She gripped the back of the chair in front of her, her knuckles white, as she searched for the right words.

"I've been sober for a lot of years," she began, her voice steady at first. "And in all that time, I've rarely felt the kind of pull I felt in the past day or so."

She paused, swallowing hard. Her eyes flicked to the faces of her group, kind and patient, before lowering to her hands. "As many of you are aware, Capri—one of my most cherished friends—was in an accident. It shook me to my core. She's okay now, but for a moment, I thought..." Her voice cracked, and she struggled to breathe. "I thought I was going to lose her."

The words came tumbling out, faster now. "And I kept thinking, if I could just do something, if I could just control the situation, maybe I could stop bad things from happening. But I couldn't. It made me feel...powerless. Scared. And for the first time in years, I thought about having a drink."

The room was silent, the weight of her words settling over the group. Reva felt tears prick her eyes. She didn't bother brushing them away.

"But I know..." Her voice softened, trembling. "I know that I *am* powerless—not just over alcohol, but over life. Over the people I love. And I have to remind myself every day that it's not my job to protect everyone. That's in God's hands."

Reva quietly recited the mantra they had all learned to cling to. "God, grant us the serenity to accept the things we cannot change, the courage to change the things we can, and the wisdom to know the difference."

She inhaled deeply, her tears spilling freely now. "One day

at a time," she whispered, her voice thick with emotion. "That's all I can do."

She sat down slowly, her hands shaking as she wiped her face. A gentle murmur of encouragement and understanding rose around her, and someone placed a hand on her shoulder. It was a small gesture, but it was enough.

12

Capri woke to the steady beep of a monitor and the antiseptic smell of a hospital room. Her eyelids felt heavy, the kind of weight that came with too many painkillers. As she blinked, the white ceiling tiles came into focus, their repetitive patterns suddenly maddening. She shifted, and a sharp pain shot through her side, causing her to gasp.

A nurse in scrubs the color of a summer sky appeared at her side. "Easy there, Miss Jacobs," the nurse said with a soothing tone. "Don't try to move too much. Remember, you've got a few broken ribs and a leg trying to heal." She pointed to the traction apparatus.

Capri blinked up at her. "How could I forget?" Her voice came out raspy, foreign to her own ears—her memory blurry and indistinct.

"That was quite the accident on that mountain," the nurse noted, checking the IV attached to Capri's arm. "Do you remember anything?"

Memories flooded back with a sickening clarity: the roar of the snowslide, the jarring impact, the desperate struggle to keep control. Capri closed her eyes and let out a shaky breath. "Yeah," she whispered. "I remember."

The nurse's kind eyes softened. "You gave us all quite a scare. But you're lucky—it could've been much worse."

Lucky. The word stung. Capri didn't feel lucky. She felt stupid. Reckless. Her body ached all over, and the weight of what could have happened pressed down on her. What did happen to other racers. She nodded absently; her throat too dry to say anything more.

The nurse adjusted Capri's blankets and fussed with a machine beside her bed. "On a scale of one to ten, how's your pain?"

Capri leaned against the stark white pillowcase. "A four, I guess."

The nurse nodded. "That's pretty good, given your injuries. Let's try to give it another half hour before we administer more pain medication. Until then, are you hungry?"

Capri shook her head no.

"Okay, but we don't want you to wait too long before you get some nutrition. I'll alert dietary services to bring a lunch tray." She lightly patted Capri's shoulder. "We'll do our best to keep you comfortable. If you need anything, just press the call button, okay?"

Capri gave a small nod and watched the nurse leave, her efficient movements leaving behind the faint smell of hand sanitizer. She turned her head to the side and winced, her ribs protesting the motion.

A bouquet of cheerful daisies and mums sat on the table beside her, along with a small card. She reached for it with her good hand, her fingers trembling as she read the neat handwriting: *Get well soon – Jake.*

Her breath hitched, and she set the card down.

Jake. He'd saved her life.

He'd also seen her at her worst, and the thought twisted her stomach. She hated being vulnerable, hated that her carelessness had led her here.

As she lay back against the pillows, another memory began to surface, the fog in her mind lifting just enough for her to piece it together. Her mother had been here—Capri could vaguely recall her sitting by the bed, holding her hand. But then she'd said she couldn't stay.

Capri's heart clenched as the words came back to her—her mother needed to return to Idaho to be with her new husband. The decision felt like a stab to her heart. Dick was gone, and now her mother—the only family she had left—had chosen a different life. She was like the wind, lost and aimless without a man to guide her.

Capri swallowed hard, the ache in her chest deepening. She really didn't have any family anymore, at least none in Thunder Mountain.

The door creaked open, and a parade of voices filtered in before she saw them—the Knit Wit ladies, a whirlwind of brightly colored sweaters and sensible shoes. Betty Dunning, the de facto leader of the group, carried a large basket overflowing with hand-knit scarves, socks, and even a stuffed owl wearing a jaunty bowtie.

"Oh, Capri, honey!" Betty exclaimed, her warm voice filling the sterile room. She set the basket on the foot of the bed, and the other two women circled her like mother hens fussing over their chick. "We were so worried about you!"

"You gave us all a fright," Dorothy chimed in. "But you're looking much better already, dear."

Capri managed a weak smile. "Thanks. I'm...still in one piece."

"Barely," muttered Oma, the group's resident truth-teller, setting a plate of cookies on the bedside table. "But you'll heal, just like my Earl did after he fell off the barn roof trying to rescue a raccoon he thought was stuck. Turned out, the raccoon was just fine—Earl, not so much. Took a while, but he was good as new. Well, except for the limp when it rained." She shook her head. "That was years before he passed, bless his soul."

Capri let out a small laugh that quickly turned into a grimace as her ribs protested. "Thanks for the perspective, Oma."

Dorothy Vaughn reached for Capri's hand, her own warm and steady. "We brought you some goodies. Knitted things for when you're feeling up to looking fabulous again, and some of Betty's banana bread."

"That bread cures everything," Betty added with a wink.

Capri looked at the basket, then at the women surrounding her. Something in her tightened, but it wasn't pain. She felt the familiar lump rise in her throat—one she hadn't felt since she was a child. Her walls, always so carefully maintained, started to crack.

She glanced around the room, her gaze lingering on the familiar faces of her friends, their concern woven into every gesture and word. Maybe family didn't always share your blood—sometimes, they were the ones who showed up with cookies and stories about raccoons, reminding you that you weren't as alone as you felt.

"I was so scared," Capri whispered, the confession tumbling out before she could stop it. "I thought I...I thought I might die out there. And it was so stupid. I didn't listen to anyone. I just had to prove something."

Tears spilled down her cheeks, hot and unstoppable. "I don't even know what I was trying to prove," she choked out, shaking her head. "I just...I didn't think."

Immediately, the women were at her side. Oma wrapped an arm around her shoulders, careful not to jostle her injuries. "Oh, honey, it's okay to cry. Let it out."

"We've all done things we regret," Dorothy said gently. "The important thing is that you're still here. And you've got people who love you."

"Life is all about learning, sweetheart," Oma added. "Sometimes the lessons come hard, but they make us stronger."

"You're a fighter," Betty said with a nod. "You've always been one. And this? This is just another chapter in your story."

Capri sniffled, her tears slowing as she looked at the wise, older women around her. Their words weren't just platitudes; they came from experience, from lives lived fully and messily. She nodded, wiping her eyes with the edge of the blanket. "Thank you. Really."

"Anytime," Oma said, squeezing her shoulder. "Now, let's see if we can get you to eat a little something. Betty, where's that banana bread?"

As the women bustled around her, Capri felt the tiniest spark of something she hadn't felt since her accident—hope. It was fragile, but it was there, nestled among the hand-knit scarves and homemade cookies. And for the first time since the accident, she let herself believe she might be okay.

13

Charlie Grace juggled a lunchbox, a water bottle, and a pair of sneakers as her daughter, Jewel, hopped around the kitchen, trying to wriggle into her pink jacket. The smell of sizzling bacon and the faint, floral tang of Jewel's detangler lingered in the air, mixing with the piney scent of wood smoke from the stone fireplace in the adjacent living room. Outside, frost still clung to the windowpanes, and the hum of the school bus echoed faintly in the valley below.

"Mom, I can't find my other mitten!" Jewel whined, her voice tinged with eight-year-old urgency.

"They're by the back door, Puddin'," Charlie Grace said, setting down the sneakers and reaching for the lunchbox lid. Her hands moved quickly, tucking a homemade peanut butter and jelly sandwich into the box next to carrot sticks and a cookie wrapped in foil. "Go grab them, or you'll miss the bus."

Jewel darted off, her socks skidding on the hardwood floor, and Charlie Grace exhaled sharply, tucking a loose strand of dark hair behind her ear. She glanced at the clock. Seven twenty-seven. Three minutes to go before bus pick-up.

The back door creaked open, letting in a sharp gust of cold

mountain air as Aunt Mo stepped in, carrying a wicker basket of fresh eggs. Her cheeks were pink from the crisp morning, and her gray-tinged hair was tucked neatly under a knitted hat. "Mornin', darling," she said, shaking the cold off her boots. "I thought I'd pop over and see if you needed an extra hand."

Charlie Grace's polite smile was automatic. She turned off the stove and plated up the bacon. "I've got it, Aunt Mo. Thanks, though."

Aunt Mo didn't bother with niceties. She planted the egg basket on the counter, her brow lifting in a way that reminded Charlie Grace of a ranch foreman inspecting the hired help. "You've always 'got it.' That doesn't mean you don't need help. When's the last time you sat down, hmm?"

Charlie Grace sighed and pressed the heel of her hand against her forehead, brushing aside the creeping tension. "Really, I'm fine. Jewel's ready, and the bus is coming. After that, I've got a schedule to keep."

"Which is exactly why you *do* need help." Aunt Mo leaned against the counter, crossing her arms. "Look, you're not Superwoman, Charlie Grace. You're runnin' this ranch, raisin' a little girl, lookin' after your dad, and keeping things from falling apart. Let me take something off your plate."

The faint rhythmic sound of wheels squeaking down the hall broke the brewing argument. Charlie Grace's father, Clancy Rivers, rolled into the kitchen in his chair, his weathered hands spinning the wheels with practiced ease. His hat, as always, sat perched at a jaunty angle, the brim shadowing his sharp, lined face. His boots—polished but worn at the edges—rested on the footplate.

"Morning, ladies," he said, his deep voice rumbling like a storm on the horizon. "What's all the fuss about?"

"Nothing, Daddy," Charlie Grace said quickly, sliding Jewel's lunchbox into her backpack.

Aunt Mo gave Clancy a knowing look. "Your daughter's stubborn as a mule. Won't let anyone lighten her load."

Clancy chuckled, the sound rich and surprisingly warm. "Runs in the family."

Charlie Grace's lips twitched at the corner, and she shook her head. "Don't start." She pointed to the table. "Your bacon and eggs are waiting."

She crouched to zip up Jewel's jacket as her father maneuvered his chair to the table.

The accident that had put Clancy in the chair was years ago, but its shadow still loomed. He'd been thrown from a horse while rounding up cattle during a thunderstorm—a freak bolt of lightning had spooked the animal. The fall left him paralyzed from the waist down and changed everything for the Rivers family.

For a long time after the accident, Clancy had been angry—at the world, at himself, and most painfully, at Charlie Grace. She'd made the hard decision to turn their sprawling cattle ranch into a guest ranch to save them from financial ruin. Clancy had resisted, calling it a betrayal of their heritage, but the mounting medical bills and dwindling income left no choice.

The battle between them had been fierce, with words thrown like daggers, but time and resilience softened the edges of their conflict. Eventually, they'd found a delicate peace. Clancy, though still resistant to change, had come to respect Charlie Grace's determination and resourcefulness.

"You know," Clancy said now, breaking into her thoughts, "Mo's got a point. You don't have to do it all on your own, Charlie Grace. Stubbornness is admirable, but it ain't practical."

She glanced at her father, his gray eyes steady but soft. He wasn't lecturing—just reminding her she wasn't alone. She straightened and gave a half-hearted shrug. "I have plenty of help. Do I need to remind anyone you hired Gibbs? I fired him after finding him in the hay with Albie's niece, and you hired him back."

Was that a grin on her father's face?

She shook her head, knowing this was an argument that couldn't be won. "Fine. I'll think about it."

Aunt Mo snorted. "She won't, but at least I'll have tried."

The sound of the school bus rattling up the lane in the distance saved Charlie Grace from replying. Jewel moved for the door, mittened hands waving. "Mom! It's here!"

Charlie Grace grabbed her backpack and slung it over Jewel's tiny shoulders. "Okay, go on. I'll watch from the porch."

She followed Jewel outside, the cold biting her cheeks as she stood on the wide front porch, waving as her daughter ran for the end of the lane and clambered onto the bus. The engine growled, and the vehicle lumbered down the icy road, leaving a faint trail of diesel in the crisp air.

As she turned to go inside, her gaze swept across the sprawling ranch. The barns stood sturdy against the pale morning light, their red paint vivid against the snow-dappled fields. Smoke curled from the chimney of the main lodge, and a distant neigh carried on the wind. A horse-drawn sleigh, loaded with hay bales stood waiting.

Gibbs stepped out of the barn, adjusting his hat before leaning against the fence. A cigarette dangled between his fingers, a thin trail of smoke drifting upward as he waited for her to join him in feeding the cattle.

The ranch was alive, humming with activity, and for a moment, Charlie Grace let herself feel the pride that came with keeping it that way.

. . .

Inside, Clancy and Aunt Mo were already bickering good-naturedly, and the familiar sound made her smile. She had her hands full, no doubt about it, but this life—messy and complicated as it was—was hers. And she wouldn't trade it for anything.

~

By mid-morning, the feeding was done, and Charlie Grace headed for her office in the lodge, brushing off hay from her jeans as she walked. The wide windows of the lodge framed the sprawling pastures beyond, but she barely noticed the view. Her mind was already on the stack of mail that waited for her.

Inside, her office smelled faintly of cedar and coffee. She sat down at her desk, flipping on her desk lamp and pulling the mail closer. The stack was thicker than usual, a mixture of envelopes in various sizes and colors.

She started with the smallest ones, tearing through a slew of utility bills—electricity, propane, and water—all higher than expected thanks to the harsh winter. She added them to a growing pile before moving on to the next set of envelopes. Veterinary invoices for the horses. Feed delivery costs. A late notice from the fencing company she'd hired last fall to replace the paddocks.

Her chest tightened as the numbers added up. She pinched the bridge of her nose, trying to push back the headache threatening to creep in.

Finally, she reached the last envelope from Thunder Mountain Savings and Loan, her bank. With a heavy sigh, she tore it open and pulled out a statement. Her heart sank as she scanned the transaction details, her stomach doing a flip when her gaze landed on a particular expenditure evidenced by a cleared check tucked inside the envelope.

A check for $500. Made out to Gibbs Nichols.

"What the hell?" she murmured, holding the paper closer.

Her father's signature scrawled across the bottom was unmistakable. Charlie Grace clenched her jaw as her cheeks flushed with anger. Gibbs Nichols—the man who always seemed to turn up like a bad penny—had somehow managed to weasel his way into her father's wallet. Again.

She set the statement down and opened her laptop, her fingers flying over the keyboard as she logged into the ranch's operating account. The balance appeared on the screen, confirming what the statement said. The check had cleared two days ago.

Charlie leaned back in her chair, the leather creaking beneath her. She stared at the screen, the tightness in her gut now a full-blown ache. The ranch's finances were already stretched thin. Which is why she'd declined loaning her ex-husband money when he'd hit her up for it the other day.

This...this was a blow they couldn't afford. And to make matters worse, her dad knew it.

Her fist curled against the desk as she thought about the arguments they'd had about Gibbs in the past. Her father always swore he wouldn't let Gibbs take advantage again, yet here was the proof in black and white.

With a heavy sigh, she closed the laptop and rubbed her temples. "Looks like we're having a little talk, Dad."

Her gaze wandered out the window, the peaceful view of the ranch doing little to calm her racing thoughts. One thing was clear—she needed to get to the bottom of this, and fast.

Charlie Grace stormed across the yard, the gravel crunching angrily under her boots as she made her way to the house. Her blood boiled with every step, the statement and check still clutched tightly in her hand. The sun glinted off the frost-tipped grass, but she barely noticed. All she could think about was Gibbs Nichols and her father's baffling decision to hand him $500 without so much as a conversation.

Arriving at the backdoor leading into the kitchen, she kicked off the snow from her boots and threw it open, stepping inside with a determined stride. Her father's wheelchair sat near the dining table, where Clancy Rivers casually worked a crossword puzzle. Aunt Mo was perched nearby, folding towels and humming to herself. Both of them looked up as Charlie Grace entered, her boots stomping on the hardwood floor.

"Dad," she snapped, holding up the bank statement like it was evidence in a trial. "You want to explain this?"

Clancy squinted at the paper and set down his pen. "What's up, sweetheart?"

"Don't 'sweetheart' me," Charlie Grace fired back. "You wrote a check to Gibbs. Five hundred dollars. Are you kidding me right now?"

Aunt Mo froze mid-fold, her expression shocked. "Clancy, tell me she's wrong."

Clancy let out a huff, rolling his wheelchair back a few inches. "Now hold on, both of you. It's not as bad as you're making it out to be."

"Oh, really?" Charlie Grace said, hands on her hips. "Because from where I stand, it looks worse than bad."

Clancy sighed and leaned back in his chair, giving Charlie Grace a patient but knowing look. "Honey, I know you're upset. But Gibbs is trying. He's always been a little...impulsive, but he's got good intentions."

Charlie Grace threw her hands in the air. "Good intentions? Good intentions don't pay the feed bill or the propane to heat the lodge and the house. And they sure as heck don't undo all the damage he's done to this family."

Clancy leaned forward, resting his elbows on his knees. "I'm not defending what he's done in the past. You know that. But people deserve second chances, and sometimes third or fourth ones. I've had my share of those, remember?"

Charlie Grace's face softened for just a second as memories

of her dad's hard-fought struggle to reconcile with her mother after a one-time indiscretion flashed through her mind. But just as quickly, the frustration surged back. "That's different. You made changes, Dad. Real ones. Gibbs just keeps screwing up and expecting everyone to bail him out."

"Maybe so," Clancy said quietly. "But you know as well as I do that holding onto all that anger isn't doing you any good. He's Jewel's father, and that little girl looks up to him like he hung the moon."

Charlie Grace flinched. It was true. Jewel adored her daddy. Which is exactly why Charlie Grace had bent as far as she had in the past. But this—well, a willow branch could only flex so far without breaking.

Clancy leaned back in his chair, watching Charlie Grace pace the room like a storm ready to break. With a sigh, he reached into his wallet, pulled out a folded check, and held it out to her. "The loan's already been paid back."

Charlie Grace stopped mid-step, glaring at the check in his hand before snatching it. She unfolded it quickly, her eyes narrowing. "It's post-dated."

"Only by a week," Clancy said calmly. "He told me he asked you for an advance and you turned him down. Raising a family comes with a lot of expenses. Besides, we both know he's good for it."

Charlie Grace let out a sharp groan, clutching the check in her hand like it might catch fire. "Mark my words, this check is going to be as good as the promise he made to be faithful."

Clancy frowned but kept his tone even. "You can always dock his wages if the check bounces."

"That's not the point, Dad," she snapped. "I have other bills to pay! I can't keep carrying him, not financially, not emotionally, not any way. Gibbs has a new wife. Let her deal with his immaturity."

Clancy sighed, the lines on his face deepening. "I get it. I do.

But Gibbs is trying, Charlie Grace. Maybe not in the way you want him to, but he's trying."

Aunt Mo, who had been quietly standing near the door with a sharp eye on Clancy, finally spoke up, her voice firm and resolute. "Charlie Grace is right, Clancy. This isn't just about a post-dated check—it's about Gibbs thinking he can take shortcuts and expect someone else to clean up after him. And you did it without even consulting her, knowing she would never agree. That's not fair to her, and you know it." She stepped closer, her gaze softening as she looked at Charlie Grace. "You've worked so hard to keep this place running, sweetheart. You shouldn't have to shoulder Gibbs' irresponsibility, no matter how 'good for it' he might be."

Clancy opened his mouth to argue, but Mo cut him off with a raised hand. "Don't. You're enabling him, Clancy. You're making it easier for him to dodge the consequences of his choices. If he wants to be a father, then he needs to step up and act like one. Charlie Grace isn't his safety net."

Charlie Grace tightened her grip on the check, thankful for the support. At least someone understood the true nature of the situation.

Mo reached out and gently touched her arm. "You have a right to be upset, honey. You're in charge here." She gave her brother a look before turning back to Charlie Grace. "Just remember, you've got a lot of people who see the work you're doing and respect you for it. You don't owe Gibbs Nichols anything."

Clancy rubbed the back of his neck and sighed, finally nodding. "Maybe you're right, Mo. Maybe I shouldn't have gotten involved."

Mo smirked, her voice softening but still sharp. "Took you long enough to figure that out." She gave Charlie Grace a wink. "Now, what do you say we leave the check on the table and go grab some potatoes from the cellar for tonight's dinner? Ain't nothing a pan of my scalloped potatoes can't make better."

Charlie Grace let out a small, reluctant laugh and tucked the check into her pocket. "Sounds like a plan. Thanks, Aunt Mo."

As they left the room together, Clancy lingered behind. "Stubborn women," she heard him mutter.

14

Capri's long-term prognosis was good but not without difficulty. She quickly learned she would not be returning home anytime soon.

"Compound fractures that require external fixation prompt a far more complicated healing process than simple breaks," Dr. McCord pointed out. She learned foreign medical terms like Steinmann pin traction, Thomas splint, Pearson attachments, intramedullary rod, and post-operative edema, among others.

To her dismay, she also discovered she'd be dismissed from the hospital and directly head to a rehabilitation center where she'd spend time in intense physical therapy to increase her weight-bearing ability and to strengthen muscles that had atrophied during her extended hospital stay. She'd progress to therapies intended to restore her range of motion, joint mobility, balance, and coordination. She'd be enduring recovery for weeks before she could even return home and resume any sense of normalcy.

The entire mess frustrated her, at best. At worst, she was a total grouch.

One evening, she was in a particularly sour mood. Jake showed up after work with some chocolate milkshakes. "A treat," he offered, leaning to brush a kiss on her forehead.

Capri glared at the milkshake, then at Jake. "Oh, perfect. Just what I need while I'm stuck in this bed, not moving—extra sugar to make sure I roll out of here instead of walk. What's next? A side of fries to really round me out?"

Jake grinned as he set the milkshake on her tray. "Well, aren't you just a delight? Here I was thinking I'd earn some points for bringing your favorite, but if you'd rather pout, I can always hand the treat off to someone at the nurse station who appreciates a good chocolate shake."

Okay, fine. She was being a pill—a big, hard-to-swallow one. But no one seemed to grasp just how excruciatingly bored she was or how utterly done she felt with all of this.

She let a tiny grin form at the corners of her mouth as she grabbed the milkshake off the tray. "Look, I might be a handful...but you have two hands."

Jake wasn't the only one keeping tabs on her.

Word spread of her foul mood faster than wildfire in a dry season, and before Capri could properly wallow, her girlfriends swept into her hospital room like a well-organized ambush—Reva with a deck of cards, Lila carrying contraband snacks, and Charlie Grace declaring, "If you're gonna be cranky, at least let us enjoy the show."

Capri exhaled heavily, reluctant to admit how thrilled she was to see them.

Visitors were far better than watching the clock tick on the wall. She hadn't done anything but lay here, poked and prodded, forced to endure bland hospital food and her own restless mind.

"You look awful," Reva announced, plopping into the chair beside the bed.

"Gee, thanks," Capri muttered, shifting against the stiff hospital sheets. "I live for your encouragement."

Charlie Grace grinned as she set a bag of kettle corn on the bedside table, the buttery, slightly sweet aroma a welcome contrast to the antiseptic air. "We heard about your cranky mood and figured we'd better intervene before the nurses staged a rebellion."

Reva crossed her legs, looking particularly proud of herself. "I've already taken steps to make sure an accident like this never happens again. I'm talking major steps."

Capri narrowed her eyes. "What kind of steps?"

"The town council met with state and U.S. Park Service officials yesterday. We're getting state-of-the-art avalanche mitigation equipment, expanded rescue teams, and—wait for it—an emergency response fund that will ensure no one has to rely on just a locator beacon and a prayer ever again."

"That's…impressive," Capri admitted, her voice sober.

Reva shrugged, but there was steel in her gaze. "The avalanche made national news, Capri. Everyone's watching. We needed to act fast."

The mention of the avalanche sent a chill through the warm room. The scent of kettle corn, the rustling of plastic snack bags, even the distant sound of beeping monitors faded as Capri's thoughts drifted.

Her voice softened. "Have they…held the funerals yet?"

A silence settled over the room, heavy and unspoken. Reva exchanged a glance with Charlie Grace, who then looked at Lila.

Reva cleared her throat and shifted in her seat. "Let's talk about something else."

Before Capri could press further, Lila reached into her oversized purse and, with a triumphant smile, pulled out a bottle of champagne, along with a set of plastic flutes. "We're going to need the nurses to get us some ice," she announced.

Capri blinked at her. "We're drinking? In a hospital?"

Charlie Grace smirked. "Of course, we are. Providing you are not on painkillers."

"I haven't taken any for nearly twelve hours," Capri quickly assured while glancing at the wall clock. A wide grin formed. "I can skip the upcoming dose. I've missed our Friday night get-togethers."

"Us too." Reva stood, smoothing a wrinkle from her skirt. "But you're limited to one glass. Wait here," she said before disappearing into the hallway. Moments later, she returned with a small bucket of ice and a can of Diet Coke in hand. "For me," she said with a pointed look.

Lila popped the cork, the soft pop echoing in the small room, followed by the fizzy rush of champagne filling the cups.

She lifted her glass. "A toast is in order."

Charlie Grace arched a brow. "A toast?"

Lila's smile widened as she looked at each of them in turn. "Yes," she said, her voice brimming with pent-up excitement. "I'm going to be a grandmother."

Capri's jaw dropped. Charlie Grace's drink nearly sloshed over the rim.

"Oh. My. Word." Reva's eyes went round. "Are you serious?"

Lila offered a smile, though it didn't quite reach her eyes. "Dead serious. Camille showed up out of nowhere after leaving school and dropped the news on me. I've been sitting with it, trying to wrap my head around everything."

Capri let out a laugh, shaking her head. "Well, that is amazing news. Guess we do have something to celebrate."

She raised her glass, a genuine smile tugging at her lips for the first time in days. Maybe she was laid up in this bed, feeling like she'd never be herself again—but life outside was still moving forward.

And that was something worth toasting to.

15

Charlie Grace stood just outside the security checkpoint of the Jackson Hole Airport. The terminal held clusters of travelers in fleece jackets and hiking boots, ski bags slung over shoulders.

Coffee warmed her hands through the Styrofoam cup as she took a sip, then lifted a hand to shield her eyes from the sunlight shining in from the tarmac, where a handful of private jets and regional planes stood against the vast mountain backdrop.

She spotted Nick Thatcher before he saw her, his easy stride unmistakable in the thinning crowd. He carried that effortless presence—broad shoulders, dark hair a little tousled, a well-cut blazer over a black tee that somehow made him look both polished and rugged at once.

When he finally lifted his gaze and caught sight of her, a grin broke across his face.

"Hey, stranger," she said, stepping forward as he dropped his bag and pulled her into a tight hug.

"Hey, yourself." His voice was warm, familiar, grounding. "Miss me?"

"Maybe." She leaned in for a kiss.

Nick chuckled, shouldering his carry-on as they headed for the exit. Once inside Charlie Grace's truck, he settled in, stretching his legs and adjusting his seat with a satisfied sigh. "It's good to be home." Then he turned his attention to her, reached across the seat, and placed his hand on her thigh. "Just so you know, I'm going to want a real kiss when we get to my house." He grinned.

So did she.

Two weeks was a long time to be apart and it was good to have him home. Sure, they'd talked over the phone frequently, especially after Capri's accident. Of course, he'd also had to tell her all about the Oscars. Still, it wasn't the same as having him with her.

"Don't take this the wrong way," he said, watching her as she started the engine, "but you look tired. You okay?"

Charlie Grace exhaled, rolling her shoulders before pulling out of the airport lot. "I'm fine. Just dealing with issues with my dad. I thought we'd gotten past a lot of this friction, but it keeps rearing its ugly head. Especially when it involves Gibbs."

Nick shot her a knowing glance. "How is your ex?"

"Needy."

The truck rumbled onto the highway, the snow-covered Tetons rising in the distance. Patches of slush lined the roadside, where the late-season sun worked tirelessly to melt winter's remnants. Dirty piles of snow receded, giving way to damp earth and the first hopeful hints of green.

"Spring's coming," she mused, tapping her fingers against the steering wheel. "Skiing is slowing down. We haven't had any guests since the holidays." She sighed. "The summer tourist season can't come fast enough."

Nick studied her for a moment before shifting slightly. "Listen, if you need a little financial help to get by until things pick up—"

"No," she cut in firmly. "I'll be fine."

Nick sighed but let it drop. "Alright. But I might have something else that could help. I ran into an old friend in Hollywood—a producer for a new show called *Treasure Pickers*."

Charlie Grace shot him a skeptical glance. "What is that? Some reality show?"

"Basically," Nick said.

She scoffed. "No offense, but those shows are anything but real."

Nick continued, unfazed. "Perhaps, but this one has enjoyed rising popularity. The show features a team of expert treasure hunters who travel the country searching for rare antiques, unique collectibles, and forgotten relics tucked away in barns, garages, and roadside shops. Their keen eye for hidden gems and historical finds often leads to surprising discoveries—and unexpected fortunes. They're looking for people to feature in different episodes. I could make a call, set something up."

Charlie Grace shook her head immediately. "No way. I don't want to be on television."

Nick chuckled. "Come on, Charlie Grace. The national exposure would be worth its weight in gold. And they pay." He let that sink in. "You could use the cash."

She hesitated, her grip tightening on the wheel. The truck rolled past a pasture where a few shaggy horses picked at the exposed grass, steam rising from their nostrils in the chilly air.

"How much do they pay?" she asked finally.

Nick grinned. "Far more than you'd expect."

Charlie Grace sighed, but a small smirk played at the corner of her lips. "Well, I'm not saying yes yet. But I'm listening."

Nick leaned back in his seat, pleased. "That's all I needed to hear."

Nick was good on his word.

Within days, he had made the right calls, cut through red

tape, and arranged everything. The production team would arrive at Teton Trails Guest Ranch in a few weeks to film an episode, shining a national spotlight on the place Charlie Grace had fought so hard to keep running.

When he told her the news, standing in the dim light of the barn, she barely heard the details at first—too distracted by the way he leaned against a post, arms crossed over his chest, watching her reaction with quiet satisfaction.

She blew out a breath. "So, just like that, it's done?"

A smile nipped at the corner of Nick's mouth. "Did you expect anything less?"

She shook her head, looking away to hide the warmth creeping up her neck. She *should* have expected it. That's who Nick was—steady, capable, a man who followed through. But it was the *way* he did things, the ease with which he always seemed to take care of her, that rattled her more than she liked to admit.

"So," he continued, stepping closer, his voice taking on that low, amused tone that always unsettled her. "What are the odds you've got something valuable up there in that attic?"

Charlie Grace smirked, crossing her arms. "Slim to none. But you know these shows—they can turn an old, rusted horseshoe into the *discovery of the century* with the right camera angle."

Nick chuckled, shaking his head. "Well, either way, you're getting paid. And if they *do* find some lost fortune, I assume you'll be buying me dinner?"

She arched a brow. "That depends. Are you asking me on a date, Thatcher?"

He leaned in just slightly, his voice dropping. "I thought I already had."

Her breath caught for half a second, but she covered it with a smirk. "Guess we'll see if you earn it."

Nick just grinned, stepping back as if he knew exactly what he was doing to her.

Charlie Grace turned toward the barn door, shaking her head, but her pulse was still kicking up in a way that had nothing to do with treasure hunting.

16

Reva wasn't exactly sure how she'd been roped into this.

Perhaps it was Capri's comment about her stress levels at the hospital or Lila casually mentioning how great yoga was for mobility as you age. "It helps maintain flexibility, balance, and strength, which are key to preventing falls and keeping joints healthy," Lila informed them.

And now here she was—standing barefoot on a thin mat in the Thunder Mountain community hall, surrounded by women who looked far too eager to twist themselves into human pretzels.

"Alright, ladies!" Lizzy Barton chirped from the front of the room, her ponytail bouncing as she adjusted her mic headset. Dressed in neon pink leggings and a matching sports bra, she radiated energy Reva could only describe as *aggressively peppy*.

"This is a gentle yoga class," Lila had promised.

Lila was a liar.

Beside Reva, Dorothy Vaughn huffed, tugging at the hem of her oversized T-shirt. "I don't see why we couldn't have done this in chairs. Chair yoga is very popular, you know."

Betty Dunning adjusted her headband, squinting at Lizzy. "I'm just saying, if I go down, someone better be ready to haul me up. Last time I got stuck in a position, it took my Harold and a snow shovel to get me out."

Lizzy clapped her hands. "Okay, ladies, let's start with *Sun Salutations*! Stand tall, reach for the sky, and breathe in all the positive energy!"

Reva lifted her arms halfheartedly while Oma Griffith, standing to her left, grumbled, "I'd rather breathe in a cinnamon roll."

Lila, naturally flexible, followed every move with ease. Reva, on the other hand, was already reconsidering every decision that had led her here.

"Now," Lizzy continued, stepping between them. "Let's flow into *Downward Dog*."

Reva bent forward, placing her hands on the mat, only to realize she had zero core strength. Even after chasing a toddler for months. From the sounds of struggle around her, she wasn't alone.

Dorothy wheezed, "If I go down any further, someone call my chiropractor."

Betty let out a loud *oof* as she attempted to shift into the pose. "This is how I looked trying to get out of my clawfoot tub last week."

Oma, in the middle of her own battle with gravity, suddenly sighed. "Well, ladies, since we're all practically folded in half, might as well tell you—my Jason's getting married."

That got everyone's attention.

Lila peeked over her shoulder. "Jason? I didn't even know he was dating."

She exchanged glances with Reva, who raised her eyebrows in her direction. Jason was certainly impulsive. After years of dating Charlie Grace, he suddenly, and without any warning, proposed to her. And in public.

Of course, Charlie Grace realized they were not a good match and soon broke off the relationship.

"He's engaged?" Reva asked Oma, trying to confirm what she'd heard.

"That's right." Oma grunted, shifting to find a more comfortable stance. "Took long enough, but my Jason finally found a woman smart enough to snatch him up." A hint of wistfulness flickered across her face as she added, "Could've been Charlie Grace, but I guess some things aren't meant to be."

"Well, that's wonderful!" Betty said, though her voice wobbled as she tried to keep herself upright.

Dorothy, still struggling to hold her half-squat, let out a breath. "Well, bless her heart. Jason's always been…a lot."

Oma beamed, oblivious. "She's an accountant—smart, capable, and lucky to have him. They met at his bookstore. They share a love of bird watching. And she adores his cat, Agatha Christie."

Betty and Dorothy exchanged a knowing glance but nodded in agreement, tucking away the truth for the sake of their friend.

Just then, the side doors burst open, and Charlie Grace came running in, her hair windblown, her cheeks flushed like she had sprinted from the ranch.

"Sorry I'm late!" she announced, dropping onto a mat near Lila and Reva.

Lizzy beamed. "Welcome, Charlie Grace! We're just moving into *Pigeon Pose*."

Charlie Grace blinked. "Yeah, I'll be skipping that."

Reva, who had given up entirely and was now just sitting on her mat, raised a brow. "What's got you so flustered?"

Charlie Grace grinned. "I have news." She paused dramatically, looking around at the group. "*Treasure Pickers* is coming to the ranch to film an episode."

For a second, there was silence. Then the Knit Wits exploded.

Betty gasped. "On your ranch? A real TV show?"

Dorothy clutched her chest. "This is the biggest thing to happen in Thunder Mountain since they remodeled the bakery!"

Oma nodded sagely. "I've watched that show. They seem to make a big fuss over nothing. TV folks love to overdramatize things."

Charlie Grace quickly nodded. "I'm counting on it. But I'm getting paid handsomely, no matter what they find."

Betty wiped her forehead with her forearm. "Well, as long as it's not bad news—like the IRS showing up or something."

Charlie Grace laughed. "Nope, just a reality show invading my barn."

Lizzy, who had been watching the exchange with wide eyes, suddenly clapped her hands. "Ladies! Let's focus! Warrior Pose!"

Reva groaned as she pushed herself off the mat. "I'd rather battle a real warrior than do this again."

Charlie Grace just laughed, stretching her arms as if she had no intention of actually participating.

Reva sighed. Maybe yoga wasn't so bad after all—especially when it came with a front-row seat to good gossip. For once, Nicola Cavendish had missed the scoop, and that alone made enduring downward dog almost worth it.

17

Lila pulled her coat tighter around her as she climbed the familiar path, her boots crunching softly over the dusting of snow that had settled overnight. The air was crisp, the kind that burned her lungs just enough to remind her she was alive, that she was still here. The trees stood tall and silent, their bare branches reaching toward a pale winter sky streaked with the last traces of sunrise.

It had been too long since she'd made this trek, too long since she'd come to talk to Aaron.

At the top, she found her usual spot—a flat rock that overlooked the valley, the town of Thunder Mountain nestled in the distance. She exhaled, watching the vapor of her breath disappear into the cold air.

"Hey, you," she said softly, brushing away a thin layer of snow before sitting down. "Sorry I haven't been by in a while. Life just...got away from me."

Lila pulled the knit cap from her head. "Between the long hours at the clinic and adjusting to the new partnership with Whit, the days blurred together. It wasn't easy at first—I'd expected to take over the clinic myself, not share it with a man who rode in from Texas with his confident swagger and big ideas."

She twisted a lock of hair. "But over time, we've found a rhythm. He challenges me, but he also respects my knowledge and dedication. And despite my best efforts to keep our relationship professional, a deeper friendship formed between us."

SHE LET the wind carry the silence between them, as if waiting for a response. Her hands curled around her knees, and she let herself imagine for just a moment that Aaron was sitting beside her, the way he used to, their shoulders touching.

"You'd like him, you know," she said, smiling to herself. "Whit Calloway. He's stubborn. Drives me nuts sometimes. Thinks he knows everything. But he's got a good heart, Aaron. And he keeps showing up for me, even when I push him away." She swallowed, feeling the lump rise in her throat. "I think I love him. It's different from the love we shared, but it's there."

The admission hung in the air, both terrifying and freeing. She had loved once before, with everything she had, and that love had been stolen from her. Allowing herself to feel it again —well, that was still the scariest thing of all.

But that wasn't why she was here.

Lila looked down, her fingers tracing the frost-covered edges of the rock. "That's not why I came up to talk." She drew in a deep breath, steadying herself. "Aaron, Camille's pregnant."

Saying it out loud made it even more real. She blinked hard against the sting of tears, shaking her head. "I never saw this coming. One minute, she's packing for college, planning her future. The next...she's looking at me with those wide, scared eyes, telling me she's having a baby."

She let out a shaky laugh, pressing her fingers against her forehead. "She's strong, Aaron. You'd be proud of her. She's got a plan—says she'll take classes online, finish her degree that way. But I know what she's giving up." Lila sighed, her heart aching. "She won't have the late-night study groups, the rush of walking across campus, the friendships that come from dorm life, the silly midnight runs for coffee and pizza." Her chest tightened. "She's trading all of that for diapers and sleepless nights." She paused. "Somehow, I always wanted her life to be different from mine."

The wind whistled through the trees, and she shivered, but she didn't move. "I know she'll be okay. I know we'll figure this out. Life seldom goes as planned—I've learned that the hard way. I thought I'd never survive losing you. But I did. And now...I've found someone else to love." She glanced toward the sky. "Camille and I can survive this, too."

She let the weight of what lay ahead settle inside her, clasping her hands together as if in prayer. "Aaron," she murmured, her voice barely above a whisper, "I don't know how much pull you have with the guy upstairs, but if you do... you might ask Him to watch over our Camille."

A sharp gust of wind rushed through the trees, rustling the branches like a whispered answer. Lila closed her eyes, willing her silent message to her late husband upward.

Then, slowly, she rose to her feet, brushing the snow from her jeans. One step at a time, she made her way down the path, back to the life that was still waiting for her. Back to Camille. Back to Whit.

And back to whatever came next.

18

Several weeks had passed since Charlie Grace had agreed to let *Treasure Pickers* film an episode at the ranch, and the days had been a flurry of preparation. Now, under a bright blue sky, with the last of winter's grip fading, she worked tirelessly to make the place presentable. The flower beds circling the main house and along the path leading to the barn were beginning to show signs of life, tiny green shoots pressing through the damp soil—glory-of-the-snow and yellow bells, the earliest bloomers in the Tetons. The scent of thawing earth mixed with the crisp mountain air as she scooped mulch from a wheelbarrow, spreading it carefully around the fragile buds.

"Mom, I think I found an old horseshoe!" Jewel's voice piped up from the other side of the barn. Her ponytail swung behind her as she ran toward her mother, brushing dirt from the rusted metal. "That's good luck, right?"

Charlie Grace wiped the back of her gloved hand across her forehead and chuckled. "If that were true, this ranch would be the luckiest place in Wyoming. I think we've got a dozen of those hanging in the barn already."

"Make that two dozen," Aunt Mo called out, carrying a heavy sack of feed toward the chicken coop. "And half of them should've been thrown out years ago."

Clancy sat comfortably in his wheelchair, soaking up the spring sunshine. His face was relaxed, his weathered hands resting on the arms of the chair as he watched them work. He hadn't said much, just sat quietly, taking it all in.

"Tomorrow's the big day!" Jewel exclaimed, hopping from one foot to the other. "The TV people will be here!"

Charlie Grace shook her head, dropping another rake of mulch into the flower beds. "I still think this is a waste of their time. They're not going to find anything valuable."

Jewel gasped dramatically, planting her hands on her hips. "Mom! It's like an Easter egg hunt! What if they find treasure?"

Aunt Mo dusted off her hands and nodded. "Exactly. And even if they don't find anything worth a fortune, we're getting paid." She gave Charlie Grace a meaningful look. "That will take a big load off you, dear."

Charlie Grace sighed, adjusting her stance. "I know. I just don't want people thinking we're some gimmicky tourist trap."

Jewel crossed her arms. "It's fun, Mom! Not everything has to be so serious."

"Fun or not," Aunt Mo added, "this kind of exposure could be good for the guest ranch. People love a story, and this place has plenty of history."

Charlie Grace opened her mouth to protest when Clancy finally spoke. "She's right, you know."

Both women turned to look at him in shock.

"What?" Charlie Grace narrowed her eyes. "Who are you, and what have you done with my father?"

Clancy chuckled. "I'm just saying, there are trunks and crates full of old stuff in that barn attic. Could be something worth a couple thousand in there."

Aunt Mo tilted her head, studying him. "You've fought

Charlie Grace on every single thing she's done with this place, and now you're all for some reality TV show digging through your things?"

Clancy shrugged, a slow smile spreading on his face. "Well, I like that show. Watch it all the time. And if it fills up those guest cabins next summer, then what's the harm?"

Charlie Grace blinked, completely taken aback. She glanced at Aunt Mo, who looked equally stunned. After all the arguments they'd had over the years about modernizing the ranch, she never thought she'd hear her father say those words.

From the very start, she'd braced herself for his usual grumbling about the whole ordeal, convinced he'd complain about the disruption and shake his head at the absurdity of it all. Instead, he sat there, calm as a lazy spring morning, not just tolerating the idea but—was that a hint of amusement on his face? The man who had fought her at every turn when she'd converted the ranch was now casually suggesting they might strike gold? It was almost too much to process.

"Grandpa's right!" Jewel bounced excitedly. "This is so cool!"

Charlie Grace exhaled, taking in the eager expressions of her daughter and aunt. And now even her father, of all people. Maybe—just maybe—this wouldn't be such a disaster after all. Certainly, Nick was on board with the idea and had gone to great lengths to line everything up.

She straightened, rubbing the small of her back as anticipation took root, pushing aside the last of her reservations. A slow smile crossed her lips as she leaned over the rake and looked up into the blue sky. As the sun bathed her face in warmth, a new feeling settled over her—anticipation.

Treasure or not—tomorrow would undoubtedly be a day to remember.

19

Charlie Grace woke before dawn. She flipped on the bedside lamp, rubbing the sleep from her eyes before pulling herself from under the downy comforter and heading to the closet. What did one even wear to a television filming?

A mix of excitement and nerves pulsed through her as she rifled through her clothes, debating between casual and polished, finally settling on a fitted denim jacket over a soft, earth-toned blouse and dark jeans—put-together but still true to her ranch roots.

After slipping into her favorite pair of boots, she stood at the mirror, sweeping on a touch of mascara and blush, then smoothing a hint of gloss over her lips. Satisfied but still buzzing with anticipation, she pulled her hair into a loose braid and headed downstairs.

She barely made it to the landing before she stopped short. There, standing in the middle of the living room, was Jewel.

Charlie Grace blinked. "Oh. Oh no."

Her eight-year-old daughter had clearly dressed herself, and the result was...a spectacle. She wore a sequined tutu over her jeans, a bright yellow T-shirt featuring a sparkly unicorn, cowboy boots—with bright pink knee-high stockings peeking over the top—and a red feather boa draped over her shoulders for added flair. Atop her head sat a tiara.

"Jewel." Charlie Grace pressed her fingers to her temple. "Honey, what are you wearing?"

Jewel beamed. "My TV outfit! I want to sparkle for the cameras."

"You look like a Vegas showgirl who got lost on a cattle drive."

Her daughter grinned. "Isn't it awesome?"

"No, ma'am." Charlie Grace gently gripped her daughter's shoulders and spun her around. "Upstairs. Aunt Mo will help you find something...less bedazzled."

"Fine," Jewel huffed, stomping up the stairs. "But if I don't look amazing, I'm blaming you."

Charlie Grace took a deep breath and turned toward the kitchen, only to be met with her father, Clancy, rolling in like he owned the place. He was wearing his Sunday best—a navy suit, bolo tie, and cowboy boots polished to a mirror shine. A custom Stetson sat perched on top of his graying head.

"Dad," she sighed. "Why are you dressed like you're meeting the president?"

Clancy puffed his chest. "Gotta look sharp for the cameras. Might get discovered. Never know when Hollywood's looking for a silver fox." He winked.

Charlie Grace pinched the bridge of her nose. "You're not being discovered. And you might want to tone it down just a little."

"Too late. Already committed."

Before she could argue, the distant sound of an engine caught her attention. Then another. And another.

Charlie Grace walked to the window and groaned. A line of cars snaked down the lane toward the ranch.

"Oh, for crying out loud." She pressed her forehead to the cool glass. "The whole town is coming. Uninvited."

The lead car, a sleek black Escalade, rolled to a stop, and Reva stepped out with Lila popping from the passenger side, camera in hand.

Charlie Grace met them in the yard, narrowed her eyes, and pointed. "I don't think filming is allowed." She glanced between her friends. "The contract clearly states—"

Lila held up the camera, determined. "I'm not facing Capri without everything captured. She hopes to get released from the rehab facility next week. Until then, she expects me to bring her the full experience."

Before Charlie Grace could protest, another car pulled up. The vehicle barely came to a stop before the door flung open and Nicola Cavendish poured out in all her nosy glory, with Wooster right behind, struggling with Sweetpea, the perpetually yappy Yorkie.

"Well, well, well!" Nicola said at full volume. "A national television crew, right here in Thunder Mountain. I thought the *Bear Country* show over in Jackson was a big deal—but this? Right here in our little town? Well, you know what this means, Charlie Grace?"

"That I'm about to develop a migraine?"

"No!" Nicola clapped her hands. "It means this ranch is about to become famous!"

The Knit Wits arrived in Dorothy Vaughn's old sedan, spilling out like they'd just rolled in from a quilting bee—arms full of tote bags, each with a thermos in hand and tins of homemade goodies.

Chatter and laughter filled the air as they adjusted their sun hats, straightened their cardigans, and bustled toward the gathering, ready to dispense wisdom, opinions, and just the right amount of small-town nosiness.

"These are for Nick," announced Betty, thrusting a goody box into Charlie Grace's hands. "He loves lemon bars."

Albie Barton hustled forward, notebook in hand, practically vibrating with excitement. "Most exciting news since—well, the earthquakes last fall! This is going to be front-page material!"

Charlie Grace barely had time to gather herself before Nick's truck pulled up. Unlike the others, he unfolded from the driver's seat, broad and unhurried, scanning the scene with the sharp-eyed calculation of someone who missed nothing. His eyes soon locked on hers in that way that always made her stomach flutter. Smiling, he strolled over and pulled her into a warm embrace.

"You ready for this?" he asked, voice low.

Charlie Grace sighed and handed him the goody box. "Do I have a choice?"

Before Nick could respond, Clancy gave him an approving nod and a firm pat on the arm. "Oh, she's ready. Right, Jewel?"

Jewel, now dressed in a slightly more appropriate outfit—emphasis on slightly—grinned up at them. "Yeah! We're gonna be on television!"

Charlie Grace leaned close and whispered. "I sure hope you've got this under control."

Nick grinned. "Trying my best."

Just then, the deep rumble of an approaching box truck echoed through the crisp morning air. The television crew had arrived. The vehicle rolled to a stop just beyond the barn, kicking up a swirl of dust. A second SUV followed, both emblazoned with the logo of the national *Treasure Pickers* show.

The truck doors flung open, and out spilled a flurry of activity. Crew members in well-worn jeans, branded jackets, and utility vests moved with precision, hauling cases of cameras, boom mics, and collapsible light stands. A man in his late forties, built like an old, retired football player but with a tech-savvy edge, adjusted his baseball cap and strode toward Nick.

His name tag read Frank Ellis, the show's lead producer and on-air host. His sun-lined face broke into a practiced, easygoing smile.

"Nick Thatcher?" he asked, extending a calloused hand.

"That's me," Nick said, shaking it firmly.

Frank glanced around at the gathering townspeople, noting how some had drifted a little too close, their curiosity getting the better of them. He exhaled through his nose and muttered, "Gotta love the enthusiasm, but we need some space to work."

Nick caught the hint and sauntered over to the crowd, hands in his pockets, wearing his easygoing but authoritative expression. "Alright, folks, I know this is exciting, but we need to give the crew some room to do their thing. Step back a little, and I'm gonna need everyone to keep it quiet while they're filming."

There were a few murmurs and reluctant shuffles, but soon enough, the line of eager onlookers shifted back, settling into place just beyond where the crew was erecting a makeshift barrier.

Aunt Mo ushered Jewel back while grabbing the handles of Clancy's wheelchair. "C'mon, Jewel, let's let the professionals do their thing."

Jewel, arms folded, let out a dramatic sigh. "Fine...but do you think they'll give me their autograph?"

Mo patted her on the shoulder. "I'm sure they will—when they get finished. And you'll still get to see everything, just from back here."

As the townsfolk waited behind the rope barrier, another figure emerged from an SUV—a petite blonde with sharp green eyes and a clipboard clutched to her chest. The woman was introduced as Tess Harper, the field director. The woman exuded an air of crisp efficiency, her dark leggings and rugged boots paired with an oversized sweater and a chunky scarf. She tucked her pen behind her ear as she surveyed the property.

"This place is fantastic," she said, turning to Nick. "You live here?"

Nick motioned toward Charlie Grace. "She does." His face filled with pride as he explained she was the owner of Teton Trails Guest Ranch, a thriving retreat nestled in the foothills of the Tetons.

"She runs the whole operation," he continued. "Guests come from all over for guided trail rides, cabin stays, and a real taste of ranch life. It's one of the best spots in the region."

Frank raised an impressed eyebrow. "That so?" He turned to Charlie Grace. "Sounds like you've built quite the place."

Charlie Grace shrugged modestly, though a flicker of satisfaction shone in her eyes. "It's been a labor of love. My dad started the ranch, and I've carried his dream forward."

Tess, the field director, jotted something in her notebook. "A working guest ranch with history? That might make for some good footage, too."

Charlie Grace chuckled. "Long as you don't expect me to put on a show."

Frank grinned. "No need. A place like this speaks for itself."

Tess tucked her clipboard under her arm before turning to a cameraman who had just finished setting up a rig. Charlie Grace was introduced to Doug, a bearded giant in cargo pants and a flannel shirt, who hoisted a camera onto his shoulder and tested the lighting. Meanwhile, their sound tech, Milo, a lanky guy with glasses and a knit cap, fiddled with a boom mic.

Charlie Grace stepped forward, brushing a loose strand of hair from her face. "If you're looking for hidden gems, there's an attic in the barn full of stuff you might want to go through."

Frank raised an eyebrow. "Attic, huh?"

She nodded. "Dad said some of it might be valuable," she shrugged, "but I'm not sure."

Tess perked up, exchanging a glance with Frank. "Attics are gold mines," she murmured, making another note.

Frank's grin widened. "Alright, then. First order of business—let's see what treasures you've got up there."

Charlie Grace shot Nick a look, a flicker of anticipation in her eyes. He smirked. "Guess we're about to find out if Clancy was right."

With that, the crew grabbed their gear, and the whole production moved toward the barn, cameras rolling, ready to unearth whatever history had been tucked away for decades.

20

The rehab center's exercise room buzzed with movement and determination. The rhythmic clank of weight machines, the steady hum of treadmills, and the occasional groan of effort filled the air, mingling with the faint scent of antiseptic and sweat. Capri gripped the padded handles of her crutches, her palms slick despite the controlled temperature of the room.

If she could manage a full lap around the therapy room today—steady, balanced, and without Jenna having to grab her—she'd be cleared for discharge.

And she was ready. More than ready.

Jenna stood close, watchful but hands-off as Capri adjusted her stance, shifting carefully to avoid putting too much weight on her injured leg. "Slow and steady," Jenna reminded. "Keep your core engaged."

"I know," Capri muttered, more to herself than Jenna. She exhaled, steadying her breath as she took the first step forward. The crutches bore most of her weight, but she still felt the strain, the deep ache in her thigh a reminder that she wasn't as invincible as she once believed.

She just wanted to go home. Back to her cabin, back to some semblance of normal life.

Back to Jake.

A hand hovered near her elbow—Jenna always within reach but never interfering unless necessary. "You can do this, Capri. Stay in control."

"I've got it," Capri muttered, determination threading through her voice. She forced her knee to bend, to cooperate, to do the job it was meant to do.

This was just another rapid to navigate. One step. Then another.

To escape the pain, she let her mind fill with thoughts of Jake.

Jake, at her bedside, his quiet strength unwavering. Jake, bringing her coffee exactly the way she liked it, the small gesture speaking louder than words. Jake, sitting with her in the quiet moments, making her feel less alone than she had in years.

After Dick died, after her mother remarried and moved away, Capri had feared there would be no one left. That she would have to face everything alone. The result was a string of bad decisions. Frankly, she'd grown sick of her inner child.

Her fingers tightened on the crutches. She held her breath and planted her leg on the stiff, scuff-marked vinyl, willing another step forward.

Once in a blue moon, people could surprise you, and once in a while, people might even take your breath away.

Despite her fears, Jake had become more than just a steady presence—he was the foundation she hadn't realized she needed. Even beyond her lifelong girlfriends. Through the long, painful days of recovery, he had been there, never wavering, never making a show of his devotion but proving it in a hundred quiet ways.

He anticipated what she needed before she could ask,

offering comfort without crowding her, strength without demanding anything in return. He had slipped into her life so seamlessly that she hadn't noticed just how much she relied on him—until now.

The idea of waking up without knowing he'd be there, of facing the world without his calm, unwavering presence, sent a pang of unease through her. She had spent so long believing she was meant to go it alone, but Jake had changed that. She couldn't imagine going back to a life without him in it.

The realization sent a shiver down her spine, equal parts sobering and comforting. For the first time, she could picture herself...getting married.

The notion hit her like an unexpected gust of wind, knocking her off balance—not physically, but in a way that rattled her more.

Marriage had never been on her radar. Too much risk. Too much potential for loss.

And yet, when she thought of Jake—his patience, his quiet humor, the way he saw her, really saw her—the idea didn't feel suffocating. It felt... solid. Steady.

Like Jake himself.

Her foot landed firmly on the last mark on the floor. Jenna's hand pressed lightly on her back in encouragement. "You did it."

Capri exhaled sharply, her grip easing. She had done it. She was going home.

And for the first time, she knew exactly who she wanted waiting for her when she got there.

∼

Capri folded the last of her clothes into the suitcase, then turned to the wall, carefully pulling down the collection of get-well cards taped beside the window. She ran her fingers over a few of them—notes of encouragement, inside jokes, words from friends who had checked in even when she tried to keep them at arm's length. One by one, she tucked them into the suitcase, pausing only to glance at the clock.

She was early. Jake wouldn't be here for another hour.

With a sigh, she sat on the edge of the bed, rolling a small stress ball between her palms. Just as she was about to stand and double-check that she hadn't forgotten anything, a timid knock sounded at the door.

"Come in," she called, expecting Jenna or one of the nurses.

The door eased open, and to her surprise, Camille stepped hesitantly into the room. The girl's brown eyes flickered with uncertainty as she hovered just inside the doorway, her fingers fidgeting with the hem of her sweater.

"Hey, Camille," Capri said, straightening. "Didn't expect to see you here."

Camille gave a small, nervous smile. "I hope I'm not interrupting. I just...wanted to drop off something."

She hesitated, then stepped forward, extending a small, wrapped box. Capri took it, the weight of it solid in her hands. "You didn't have to do that."

Camille shrugged. "I wanted to."

Capri peeled away the paper, lifting the lid to find a small compass nestled in a bed of tissue paper. The brass casing gleamed under the fluorescent lights, the needle inside pointing steadily north.

Capri turned it over in her palm, a lump forming in her throat. A compass. A way forward. A reminder that no matter how lost she felt, she could always find her way.

"This is..." she cleared her throat, running her thumb over the smooth metal. "It's perfect. Thank you, Camille."

Camille gave another small shrug, but her expression was shadowed, as if she were carrying something heavier than words. Capri didn't notice it at first, but when Camille shifted, the baggy fabric of her sweater pulled tight across her stomach.

Camille immediately saw Capri looking and folded her arms over her belly, her face turning a deep shade of red. "It's not—I mean, I know it's obvious," she stammered, eyes darting to the floor. "I wasn't sure if Mom told you."

Capri's voice was gentle as she nodded. "Why are you hiding it?"

Camille's throat bobbed with a hard swallow. "Because I—" She exhaled, shaking her head. "I know I've let a lot of people down."

Shame.

Capri knew that weight, the way it curled around your ribs and made you feel like you were sinking. But looking at Camille—young, scared, already bracing for judgment—she felt something else stir. Compassion. Fierce and unwavering. Because if Capri had learned anything, it was that mistakes didn't define a person—how they chose to move forward did.

Capri took a slow breath, setting the compass aside before leaning forward. "Camille, listen to me. No matter how we break the rules we make for ourselves, no matter how many times we stumble, we keep moving forward. We throw tantrums when things don't go our way. We whisper secrets with our best friends in the dark. We look for comfort where we can find it. And sometimes, against all logic, against all experience, we fight it."

Camille's eyes shone with unshed tears. Capri held her gaze, steady and sure.

"You fight it. You fall. And it's scary as hell." She paused, letting the weight of those words settle. "But you know what? There's an upside to free-falling—it's the chance you give your friends to catch you."

Camille swiped at her cheek. "I don't know if I deserve that."

Capri smiled softly. "You do. You always will."

For a long moment, Camille stood there, as if letting the words soak in. Then, with a shaky breath, she nodded.

"Thank you," she whispered.

Capri squeezed her hand. "Anytime, kid."

Capri exhaled, letting Camille's words settle between them before tilting her head. "So... what's it like? Being pregnant?"

Camille blinked at her, surprised by the question. "Oh. Uh...weird." She let out a small laugh. "I mean, I'm sick all the time, and smells that never bothered me before suddenly make me want to hurl. But..." She hesitated, a shy smile forming. "It's kind of exciting, too. Like, there's this little person growing inside me, and no matter how scared I am, I already love them."

Capri studied her for a beat, then smiled. "Got a name picked out yet?"

Camille shook her head. "Not yet. I don't even know the gender." She hesitated before adding, "But if it's a girl, I've been thinking about Ella. And if it's a boy...maybe Aaron." She paused, her eyes filling with emotion. "After my dad."

Capri nodded, considering. "Good names. Strong names." Then she grinned mischievously. "Or maybe you'll have twins."

Camille groaned, eyes widening in horror. "Don't even say that."

Capri chuckled and reached for her suitcase again. "Fine, fine. But just know that if it happens, I get full 'I told you so' rights."

Camille rolled her eyes. "Yeah, well, if that happens, I'm handing one over to you."

Capri froze mid-zip, then turned to Camille, dead serious. "I take it back. You'll have one perfect, singular baby."

21

Frank Ellis, the lead producer and show host, adjusted the brim of his cap as he ascended the rickety wooden stairs into the attic of the Teton Trails Guest Ranch barn. The old structure groaned beneath his weight, dust motes swirling in the golden light that filtered through the gaps in the weathered siding. The scent of aged timber, dry hay, and lingering traces of livestock filled the air, mingled with the musty aroma of time long past.

Behind him, Tess, the field director, moved with careful precision, clipboard in hand, while Doug, the bearded giant in cargo pants and a flannel shirt, hoisted a camera onto his shoulder, testing the lighting.

The barn's loft was packed tight with stacks of trunks, old wooden crates, and cardboard boxes with their edges curled from years of neglect. Milo, the lanky sound tech with glasses and a knit cap, adjusted his boom mic, ensuring he captured every creak of the wooden planks beneath their feet.

Charlie Grace followed, her boots kicking up tiny clouds of dust. As she reached the top, her gaze flickered to a pile of hay near the far wall. A bitter memory resurfaced—finding Gibbs tangled up with Lizzy right there, their hushed whispers and guilty faces still burned in her mind. She gave herself a small shake. Not today.

From below, Clancy's voice rang out, full of excitement. "Start with those trunks, the old ones near the back wall! Those have been up there since before I bought this place!" His wheelchair was parked at the bottom of the stairs, his head tilted upward, watching the scene unfold. "It all belonged to old man Alf Morgan. He died years ago. I bought this ranch from his estate. The only heir was his daughter, but she passed away some time ago. I saw her obituary in the Cheyenne newspaper —died a childless old maid."

Charlie Grace winced at his careless phrasing. She made a mental note to bring it up with him later. For now, she shifted her attention back to the task at hand.

Frank knelt beside a stack of dusty trunks and old boxes, then pried open the first with careful hands. The leather straps cracked as he unfastened them, the metal buckles tarnished with age. Inside lay a collection of rusted tools, an old miner's lantern, and a bundle of faded letters tied with a frayed ribbon. He held up the lantern with a grin. "Classic carbide miner's lamp. Not worth a fortune, but still a great find."

Tess nodded, making notes as the camera rolled, capturing her and Frank. "We'd be willing to offer two hundred for the set."

The camera rolled to Charlie Grace. Still caught up in the moment, she nodded without hesitation. "Wow. That's great!"

Before the words fully left her mouth, Nick leaned in, whispering, "You know you're allowed to haggle, right?"

She shot him a quick smirk but made a mental note to be more mindful.

Another box revealed a tin full of old silver dollars, their faces worn smooth from handling. Frank examined a few, flipping them in his hand before making another offer, which

Charlie Grace quickly accepted. Nick sighed but chuckled under his breath.

Then they moved to the big trunk.

It sat toward the back of the attic, half-buried beneath a pile of burlap sacks. The wood was dark, almost black with age, the iron reinforcements still sturdy despite the rust creeping along their edges. A thick padlock held it shut, its keyhole filled with dust and time.

"Do you have the key?" Tess asked.

Charlie Grace moved to the stairs and looked down, spotting her dad sitting in his wheelchair. "Dad, do we have a key to that old trunk?"

He shook his head and hollered. "Afraid not."

Charlie Grace returned to the trunk and delivered the news. "I guess you can break the lock open."

Frank nodded with a grin. "Won't be the first time." He motioned to Milo who slipped a bolt cutter from his back pocket and handed it over.

Charlie Grace ran her hand over the lid. "Go ahead," she said, stepping back.

With a few well-placed strikes, Frank cut through the lock, sending sparks flying. Doug zoomed in with the camera as the lid creaked open. Inside, beneath a layer of yellowed fabric, lay stacks of black-and-white photographs, their edges curled with age. The images depicted men and women in old-fashioned clothing, standing on what appeared to be the deck of a ship.

Clancy called up from below. "What did you find?"

Charlie Grace sifted through the pictures. "Photographs. Looks like an immigrant family arriving by boat," she said in a voice loud enough for him to hear.

Clancy let out a short laugh. "Must be Alf's family in those pictures."

As they carefully sifted through the trunk, Tess reached in and pulled out a small velvet pouch, its drawstring nearly rotted away. With the utmost care, she eased it open, revealing something gleaming inside.

The cameraman came in closer.

Frank lifted the item into the dim attic light—a gold pocket watch, its casing ornately engraved. He turned it over, his eyes widening. "Do you know what you have here?" His voice carried an edge of disbelief as he looked at Tess. "Oh, my goodness. This is a Patek Philippe."

Charlie Grace exchanged looks with Nick, unsure of the significance.

Frank exhaled slowly, his voice barely above a whisper. "Not just any Patek Philippe. This could be one of the rarest models in existence."

From below, Clancy shouted, "What did you find?"

Tess ran her fingers over the watch's face, her breath hitching. "If this is authentic, it could be worth..." She trailed off, then locked eyes with Charlie Grace, gripping her arm. "This watch is valued at about ten million dollars."

Milo's boom mic wobbled in his grip. Even Doug's camera shook slightly as he zoomed in on the gleaming watch.

Silence swallowed the attic, thick and weighty. Charlie Grace's pulse pounded so fiercely she could hear it in her ears, feel it in her fingertips as they clamped onto Tess's arm.

Nick stared at the watch, then at her, his mouth parting slightly in stunned disbelief.

"That's..." He let out a low whistle, raking a hand through his hair. "That's ten *million* dollars." A slow grin spread across his face, his eyes shining with something close to wonder. "Charlie Grace. You just hit the jackpot."

Her breath caught, the weight of it all pressing against her ribs. But then Nick let out a laugh, shaking his head in amazement as he pulled her into an embrace. "You ready to be Wyoming's newest millionaire?"

Realization crashed over her like a rogue wave, stealing her breath. That sum was enough to pay off the ranch loan. Enough to erase every sleepless night spent worrying about money. Enough to change everything.

From below, Clancy's voice bellowed once more—this time a bit louder. "Would somebody please tell me what the hell is going on up there?"

22

Charlie Grace stood just outside the barn, arms folded, watching as Frank Ellis, the *Treasure Pickers* host, held the old pocket watch delicately in his gloved hand. His voice was filled with awe as he turned the timepiece over, showing off the fine engravings to the crew.

"I put in a few calls, and this is the real deal," Frank said, his tone tinged with reverence. "An 1870s Patek Philippe minute repeater. These were owned by some of the wealthiest people back then—railroad tycoons, industrialists, maybe even royalty." He let the thought hang while watching Charlie Grace for her reaction. "Of course, we'll have to have an appraisal done before we cut you a check, so to speak. But I hope you understand what just happened here." He gently placed the watch in her hand.

Charlie Grace's heart raced. She had always known there was junk hidden in her family's old barn, had even planned to have it all hauled out of there, but the task never became a priority. How could she have guessed this—this treasure, this rare piece of history—was among all the junk?

Clancy Rivers, positioned in his wheelchair nearby, looked just as stunned as she felt. His broad hands gripped his knees tightly, his gaze locked on the watch as though it might vanish if he blinked. "I can't believe it," Clancy muttered, his voice hoarse. "I thought all those trunks were filled with just some old scraps."

Frank smiled at him, clearly enjoying the moment. "You'd be amazed how often that's the case. But this right here? It's worth more than most folks could imagine."

Tess, the field director, stepped in close and signaled to the cameraman. "Clancy, can you hold it up for a second?" she asked, her voice calm but intent. She motioned for Charlie Grace to join him. "We need to get a shot of the two of you holding it, really let it sink in."

Clancy nodded, though his hands trembled slightly as he took the watch. His face shifted from disbelief to awe, the weight of the moment settling in. He turned the watch over carefully, tracing the engraving with a finger.

Frank leaned in. "Those markings are key." He shook his head. "It's authentic."

Charlie Grace couldn't help but smile, despite the storm of emotions swirling in her chest and all the cameras pointed at her. "I never knew the watch was in there," she said, her voice steady but filled with wonder. "It's just been sitting in that trunk for decades."

Frank laughed, the sound rich with excitement. "That's what we love about this show. People have no idea what they're sitting on." He turned to the crew. "This is what we live for."

Charlie Grace caught sight of Nick just beyond the boundary, standing tall with that easy, knowing grin of his. Arms crossed, his blue eyes locked onto hers, radiating nothing but pride. No teasing, no jokes—just pure, unfiltered happiness for her. The weight of the moment pressed against her chest, and for the first time since this whirlwind began, she felt steady. He gave her a small nod, the kind that said '*I see you. You earned this.*' And just like that, the chaos around her faded, if only for a second.

Tess looked up from her clipboard, her brow raised with curiosity. "So, what does this mean for you, Charlie Grace?"

The question stilled the air for a moment, and all eyes turned to her. She swallowed, her mind spinning with the possibilities. She'd always joked about how she'd like to be rich but never expected the word would be associated with her name.

"It means a lot of things," she said, finally. "It means I need to sit down before I fall over." She plopped onto the hay bale beside Clancy, exhaling.

A ripple of laughter spread through the crew, but Charlie Grace wasn't done.

She shook her head. "It also means my bank account might finally forgive me for all those times I've whispered, 'Hold on, baby, we'll get through this.'"

The laughter grew louder.

Charlie Grace ran her fingers over the intricate engraving on the watch, her expression softening. "It also means my family will no longer just be...getting by." She swallowed, feeling the weight of that realization. She put her hand on her dad's knee. "I guess it means we have a whole lot of figuring out to do."

Charlie Grace watched as Clancy stared at the watch, his weathered hands flexing against his knees like he wasn't sure whether to laugh or cry. His face, normally as solid and unshakable as the Tetons, shifted—his mouth pressed into a hard line, his throat working against emotion he wouldn't dare let loose in front of a crowd.

She squeezed his knee, grounding them both. "Dad?"

He let out a slow breath, shaking his head like he still couldn't believe it. "Your mama would've loved to see this day," he said, his voice thick, rough around the edges. Then, after a beat, he gave a gruff chuckle, blinking fast. "Though she'd probably tell us not to go gettin' big heads about it."

Charlie Grace felt a laugh bubble up, unexpected but welcome. "She'd tell us to be smart," she murmured, rubbing her thumb over the back of his hand. "And not to do anything dumb."

Aunt Mo let out a low whistle, hands on her hips as she eyed the watch. "Well, sugar, I'd say the good Lord finally decided the Rivers family was due for a blessing."

Before Charlie Grace could respond, Jewel scrunched up her nose and piped up, "Does this mean we're getting a hot tub? 'Cause my legs been real tired lately."

Beyond the makeshift boundary the *Treasure Pickers* crew had set up, the gathered townspeople buzzed like a hive of restless bees. Word had spread fast—something big had been found in the barn—and now half of Thunder Mountain seemed to be here, craning their necks, standing on tiptoes, whispering and speculating.

Nicola Cavendish, always one to sniff out a story before it was even fully baked, clutched her rhinestone-studded phone in one hand and her freshly groomed Yorkie, Sweetpea, in the other. "A Patek Philippe," she repeated to the woman beside her, widening her eyes for dramatic effect. "Do you know what that means, Dorothy? That's European royalty-level money. Charlie Grace could be—heavens—*rich* rich." She let that settle before sucking in a sharp breath. "And to think, she's been riding around town in that old truck of hers. Imagine what she can drive now."

Her husband, Wooster, the town's ever-practical banker, let out a heavy sigh and adjusted his tie. "Well," he finally grumbled, arms crossed, "if she's smart, she'll invest it. Not go blowin' it on nonsense like some people." His pointed glance at Nicola and her jeweled shoes did not go unnoticed.

"Excuse me?" Nicola snapped, flipping her highlighted hair over her shoulder. "I happen to invest in quality." She gave Sweetpea's matching pearl collar a little tug as proof.

Albie Barton had already pulled a notepad from his pocket and was furiously scribbling. "I'm not sure there's ever been a bigger story. Literally. We could be talking museum-level significance. Thunder Mountain itself could end up on the map."

"Well, it's already on the map, Albie," Pastor Pete's wife, Annie, chimed in with a chuckle, "but I get what you're sayin'."

Brewster Findley poked Gibbs' side with his elbow. "Guess you should've stayed married." A few folks chuckled, and Gibbs, ever the smooth talker, just smiled. "Didn't know we were sitting on a gold mine," he said, his tone easy, but his eyes flicked toward Charlie Grace with something unreadable—calculation, maybe.

Lizzy nudged him playfully. "Too late now. You're taken."

Gibbs laughed, but Charlie Grace didn't miss the way his fingers twitched at his side, as if counting the dollars that had slipped through them.

Across the way, a few ranchers in dusty boots murmured among themselves, shaking their heads in amazement. "Can't believe it," one of them muttered. "That ol' barn's been standin' there forever. Who would've thought?"

As the murmurs swelled, Nicola leaned in toward her husband, voice dropping to a whisper but still loud enough for half the crowd to hear. "Wooster, you will make sure Charlie Grace deposits every dime of that into the bank, won't you?"

Reva sighed, already exhausted by the inevitable chaos this find would bring. "Nicola, for the love of all things holy, please do not harass Charlie Grace about her finances."

Nicola huffed but kept her gaze locked on Charlie Grace, who was still deep in conversation with Frank Ellis. "I'm just sayin'...somebody's got to guide her through this. And who better than Wooster?"

Behind her, Sweetpea let out an indignant yip, as if in agreement.

∼

WITHIN HOURS, appraisers confirmed what the television crew had expressed.

Ten million dollars. A Patek Philippe pocket watch, hidden away in a rusted tin box buried beneath the old feed sacks, now confirmed as one of the rarest in the world. And she—Charlie Grace Rivers—was suddenly, inexplicably, rich.

This wasn't supposed to happen. People like her—people who worked sunup to sundown just to keep the ranch afloat—didn't stumble into wealth overnight.

She thought about her father, Clancy, who was napping on the porch back at the main house, completely worn out by the morning and all that followed. Did he truly understand the seismic shift this discovery meant in their lives? Would she even believe it once the shock wore off?

"Charlie Grace?"

She turned sharply at the sound of her name. Nick stepped from the barn's doorway and headed in her direction, his broad frame backlit by the afternoon sun, his expression careful. He'd been there through the entire evaluation, standing by her side, a steadying force in a day that had flipped her world upside down. She saw the concern in his eyes, the way he studied her like he expected her to crumble any second.

She let out a laugh as he neared—high and strange, a little bit wild. "Nick. I'm rich."

His lips lifted slightly. "Yeah, babe. You are."

A sob broke free before she could catch it, and suddenly, the weight of it all slammed into her. Ten million dollars. Enough to fix everything. The guest ranch. Clancy's endless medical bills. The leaking roof. The worn-out tack room. The late invoices from suppliers she'd barely managed to stay ahead of. It wasn't just money. It was freedom.

Nick crossed the remaining space in three long strides, his hands bracing her shoulders, warm and solid. "Hey. It's okay."

She wiped at her cheeks. "I don't know what to do."

"You don't have to know yet. One step at a time."

She pulled in a shaky breath, nodding. But already, her mind was racing. The taxes. The security risks. The vultures that came out of the woodwork when money was involved. The town's reaction. How long before everyone treated her differently? How long before Gibbs showed up with his hand out, smooth-talking and scheming?

Nick seemed to read her thoughts because his grip on her tightened slightly. "You don't owe anyone anything, Charlie Grace. This doesn't change who you are."

She searched his face. "Doesn't it?"

He exhaled. "Only if you let it."

A fresh wave of emotion crested over her, but this time, it was steadier. There was power in knowing she had choices now, that she wasn't backed into a financial corner at every turn. But there was also fear—fear of what it would mean to step into this new reality, to be a woman with wealth when all she'd ever known was struggle.

"I need to sit down," she muttered.

Nick guided her to an overturned crate, settling beside her, his presence grounding. They sat in silence for a long moment, the scent of hay and old wood wrapping around them like a familiar embrace.

Finally, she let out a long breath. "I don't want to lose myself in this."

He nodded. "Then don't. Stay who you are. Stay Charlie Grace."

She swallowed past the lump in her throat, lifting her gaze to meet his. "Will you help me?"

Nick's expression softened. "Always."

And for the first time since the appraisers had confirmed the impossible, Charlie Grace exhaled, steadying herself against the weight of it all—not as something overwhelming, but as a gift she was ready to carry.

23

The fire crackled in Capri's stone hearth, casting a warm glow across the newly renovated living room. The sage green and creamy white furniture was arranged in a way that encouraged conversation—something Jake had been mindful of when designing the space. Not that Capri would easily admit it aloud, but she appreciated his thoughtfulness more than she let on.

As if reading her mind, Jake set down the tray of drinks on the coffee table and pressed a quick kiss to Capri's temple before grabbing his jacket. "I'll let you girls have your time," he said, flashing his easy grin. "Call me if you need anything."

Capri rolled her eyes at his overprotectiveness, but she couldn't shake the warmth spreading in her chest as she watched him leave.

Charlie Grace barely suppressed a smile from her spot on the couch, swirling her wine glass. "He's been hovering, huh?"

"You have no idea," Capri muttered, stretching out her legs —her right one still stiff but healing well. "I can finally move without wincing, and yet he still insists on carrying everything for me, like I'm made of glass."

Lila frowned. "Give him a break. You're still on crutches."

Reva laughed, tucking her legs under her as she leaned back. She cupped a mug of chamomile tea in her hand. "Enjoy it while it lasts. That man is smitten with you."

"Yeah, yeah," Capri said, brushing off the remark, though her cheeks betrayed her with a telltale flush. She placed her glass down a little too hard, a tiny drop sloshing over the side. "I never said I *don't* like Jake's attention," she muttered, dabbing at the spill with a napkin. When she looked up, three pairs of eyes were locked on her, grinning. "Oh, shut up. All of you."

Lila lifted her wine glass in Capri's direction with a teasing smirk. "Well, I can tell you that having someone dote on you isn't the worst thing." She sighed. "You're just like my daughter. Camille barely lets me fuss over her."

Charlie Grace set her wine down. "How's she doing with everything? Is she excited yet?"

Lila exhaled, shaking her head. "I wish I could say yes. She's handling things, doing well in her online classes, but...I don't know. I just don't feel like she's letting herself feel it yet."

"She still doesn't want to know if it's a boy or a girl?" Capri asked.

"Nope. Not yet. She says she might change her mind, but honestly, I think she's still wrapping her head around the whole thing. We went maternity shopping, and she was picking things out, but it felt more like she was going through the motions." Lila reached for a piece of cheese from the platter on the coffee table. "I know she's scared. I just wish she'd let herself get excited. Because I am."

Reva squeezed Lila's hand. "She'll get there. It's a lot to process. Babies make everything feel real in a way nothing else does."

Charlie Grace raised a brow. "Speaking from experience?"

Reva let out a dry chuckle. "Let's just say they are cute as babies. But the toddler years?" She mock-shuddered. "That's when the real work starts. That's when you wonder if you've ruined them or if they'll end up on a therapist's couch complaining about you one day."

Lila chuckled. "Well, that's comforting. Although the same can be said about teenagers."

As the group's laughter faded, Capri leaned back with a sly grin, tilting her wine glass toward Charlie Grace. "Enough about me—let's talk about you, Miss Sudden Fortune," she teased, and just like that, all three women turned their attention to Charlie Grace, eyes gleaming with curiosity and mischief, ready to dissect every detail of her newfound wealth.

Charlie Grace leaned forward, refilling her glass with a sigh. "Well, it's done. The watch is officially sold. The transaction closed last Tuesday."

Lila's brows lifted. "Just like that?"

"Just like that." Charlie Grace took a slow sip, letting the words settle before grinning. "And you would not believe the way people are acting ever since the pocket watch discovery. I thought maybe a few folks would have questions, but the whole town has lost their minds."

Capri gave her a wolfish grin while stretching out her recovering leg. "Oh, I believe it. Let me guess—Nicola Cavendish has already called dibs on whatever donations you'll be making. Goodness knows, she has a long list of favorite community events."

"Oh, she was first in line," Charlie Grace said, setting down her glass with a flourish. "Stopped me in the post office, Sweetpea yapping in her arms, and whispered, 'I nominated you for Woman of the Year at the chamber luncheon.'"

Reva choked on her tea. "Are you serious?"

"As a heart attack," Charlie Grace said. "Like I want some fancy award I didn't even ask for."

Reva dabbed at her mouth with a napkin, still recovering from her near tea disaster. "Okay, hold on—I do think you deserve that award," she said, pointing at Charlie Grace. "But let's be real, Nicola didn't nominate you out of the goodness of her heart. That woman's buttering you up like a biscuit at a Sunday brunch."

Lila laughed, shaking her head. "Sounds like Nicola is in rare form. I can only imagine what the others are saying."

"Oh, it seems the entire town has reached new levels of crazy. Everyone's laying it on thicker than a fresh coat of paint. It's like I went from Charlie Grace to Queen Charlie, and I hate it."

Charlie Grace shifted, fixing her friends with a sharp look. "The Knit Wits ambushed me at the Moose Chapel quilting circle. Oma Griffith set down her crochet hook, folded her hands like she was about to pray, and said, 'Charlie Grace, honey, we're just wondering—what exactly does a person do with that kind of money?'"

Reva gasped. "What did you tell her?"

Charlie Grace barely missed a beat, flashing a dry smile. "Oh, you know, the usual—buy a yacht, fund a llama sanctuary, maybe build a gold-plated outhouse just to see if I can."

They all shared a laugh.

"Good to see you're not losing your sense of humor," Lila noted.

"Truth is, the money is not all mine. We're in the process of setting up a trust for Jewel, with protections that will keep Gibbs' mitts off the money. Another third is Dad's. He intends to pay off all the ranch loans and wants to purchase old man Johnson's property to the west." She folded her feet up under her on the sofa. "And get this—he wants to expand the guest ranch. Build new guest quarters. Put in a tennis court, a golf course, and a pool!"

Reva's hand went to her chest. "No! Are you kidding? The man who fought the guest ranch concept because he didn't want the cattle ranch he built to change?"

"No one is more surprised than I am," Charlie Grace said, eyes twinkling. "Then Oma Griffith gave me some sage advice. She caught me in the grocery store aisle, leaned in—hand to her chest, mind you—and said, 'Charlie Grace, dear, you must be careful. Wealthy women get targeted. People will want things." She lowered her voice. "Men will want things.'"

Reva let out an exaggerated sigh and set her cup down on the table. "Well, in that case, we should retroactively invoice every man we've ever dated."

Capri laughed. "Yet I don't think Oma was completely off in her advice. I'm not ultra-rich, but I have a little money. Believe me, you'll become a magnet for all the gold diggers."

Charlie Grace nodded and tapped her wine glass with an hors d'oeuvre spoon. "Ding, ding, ding. And then, as if summoned by the forces of pure irony, Gibbs Nichols walked into the store and had the audacity to say—and I quote—'Hey, Charlie Grace, about your new windfall. We should grab dinner. Talk about some investment ideas I have.'"

Capri groaned. "Of course, he did."

"Yes, he did," Charlie Grace echoed. "And before I could shut him down, Oma turned right around and muttered, 'See? Told you so.'"

The women erupted into laughter, Reva wiping a tear from her eye. "I swear, Gibbs could smell money from across state lines."

"Oh, he's not even pretending to be subtle," Charlie Grace said. "I caught him cornering Clancy yesterday, asking if we were looking for an advisor to help 'manage our affairs.'"

Lila blinked. "Gibbs? A financial advisor?"

Charlie Grace lifted her glass. "He couldn't manage a checking account without over-drafting. He just wants another handout. Probably thinks I'll finance his next failed business venture."

More laughter spilled through the room as Charlie Grace

shook her head. "But honestly, it's not just Gibbs. My ranch hands all thought I was going to sell and retire. I walked into the barn, and they were literally taking bets on where I'd move. Jackson Hole, Montana, the South of France—"

Reva's eyebrows shot up. "The South of France?"

"I know, right?" Charlie Grace grinned. "Then Ford Keaton, the most practical of the bunch, goes, 'Nah, she's not going anywhere. She's too stubborn.'"

"He's not wrong," Capri said.

"Nope," Charlie Grace agreed. "So, then the next logical thing they start betting on? What's the first thing I'll spend money on. They all assumed I'd get some massive fancy horse trailer, a new truck, maybe even a big new house in Jackson."

Charlie Grace sighed dramatically. "My actual money pit is Clancy Rivers. Dad sits at his computer all day, ordering every single thing he's ever wanted but never let himself buy."

Reva grinned. "Uh-oh. What's he gotten so far?"

"Let's see," Charlie Grace said, ticking them off on her fingers. "Three different drone kits, a leather recliner that massages, high-thread-count silk bedsheets, and some ridiculous pairs of noise-canceling headphones—"

"Plural?" Capri asked.

"Oh, multiple pairs," Charlie Grace confirmed. "He says he needs a backup in case one malfunctions."

Lila chuckled. "I take it the Amazon packages keep coming?"

"Like clockwork. My driveway looks like a fulfillment center. If I let this go on much longer, he'll have the whole house looking like a Walmart."

Reva smirked. "So, what was the first thing you bought?"

Charlie Grace shrugged. "A fancy espresso machine."

Capri lifted her glass. "Now that is a worthy investment."

Charlie Grace laughed. "Darn right." She shook her head. "Don't get me wrong, this windfall is a huge blessing. But I don't want a big deal made of it. Rest assured, none of the important things in life will change."

The conversation settled for a moment, warmth filling the space between them. Capri leaned back and gave a soft smile. "I really have missed these nights."

Reva sighed contentedly. "Same."

Charlie Grace nudged Capri. "And I have to say, for all your complaining, you seem to be enjoying having Jake around."

Capri rolled her eyes but couldn't quite suppress her smile. "He's fine."

Reva snorted. "Fine? The man basically moved in to take care of you."

Charlie Grace grinned. "And now that you're healing, what happens next?"

Capri hesitated, eyes flicking toward the door Jake had walked out of earlier. "I don't know," she admitted, swirling her wine. "But for the first time in a long time, I'm willing to find out."

Reva lifted her glass. "To figuring things out."

Lila clinked hers against it. "And to not murdering pregnant daughters during their hormonal phases."

Reva groaned. "Amen to that."

As the laughter filled Capri's newly finished home, she felt it—not just the comfort of old friendships, but the quiet hum of something new.

And for once, she wasn't running from it.

24

Charlie Grace cradled the warm mug of coffee in both hands, inhaling the rich aroma as she stood at the kitchen window in her bathrobe. The morning light spilled golden over the pine tops beyond the meadow, a peaceful contrast to her past couple of days. The closing was done, the ink dry. Very soon, they would pay off the mortgage and own the guest ranch free and clear.

No more financial worries. No more pouring over the cash flow hoping for magic. No more sleepless nights trying to dream up yet another way to stretch their dollars.

Instead, she could focus on what she loved—her guests, her horses, and the land—without the constant worry. It was freeing, exhilarating even. For the first time in a long time, she felt light. Happy.

And it was all because Nick had nudged her toward this opportunity, believing in her even when she hesitated. Without him, none of this would have happened. Just one more reason she was falling for the man who always seemed to know exactly what she needed before she did.

A strange noise caught her attention, breaking into the quiet. She cocked her head, frowning.

Then the shouting started.

Charlie Grace stiffened, her heart kicking up a notch. Shouting wasn't exactly unusual around a working guest ranch —wranglers hollered at stubborn horses, and the occasional ranch hand let out a curse when a boot met a stray pitchfork— but this was different. Urgent. Chaotic.

She set down her coffee mug and strode toward the back door, wiping her hands on her bathrobe. As she reached for the knob, another burst of voices rang out, overlapping, the tone unmistakable now—demanding, insistent.

Reporters.

Charlie Grace spun on her heel and bolted up the stairs, taking them two at a time. In her room, she yanked open her dresser, grabbed the first shirt she saw, and tugged it over her head, hopping into a pair of jeans before shoving her feet into her boots. No time for finesse—just fast, just necessary.

She ran a hand through her hair, barely taming the wild waves, then hurried back down, her pulse hammering. Without missing a beat, she strode back to the kitchen with her mind racing.

She could order them to vacate her private property, but she supposed they'd only corner her somewhere else. At least here at the ranch she had some control of the situation.

Bracing herself, she took a deep breath and swung open the back door—

Only to find Jewel in her pink-striped pajamas, standing atop the porch railing, arms flung wide like a conductor before an orchestra of news cameras.

"—and let me tell you, it wasn't that long ago when every time I asked for something—new shoes, a snack at the store, even just a little treat—Mom would sigh and say, 'Not this time, sweetheart. Money's tight.' It felt like everything was too expensive, and no matter what, the answer was always no."

Cameras. Reporters. A veritable flood of news vans lined the driveway, their satellite dishes pointed skyward like giant robotic vultures. Boom mics bobbed over her daughter's head, lenses zoomed in.

Jewel grinned. "This is like a big ol' Christmas present, and I know EXACTLY what I want—Lottie dolls! Lots of 'em!"

Charlie Grace lunged forward, hauling her daughter off the railing before she took a dive into morning show infamy.

"Jewel Rose, get inside. Right now."

"What? I was just—"

"Inside." Charlie Grace propelled her through the doorway and shut the door firmly. "Rule number one, young lady: Do not air family finances to a horde of hungry reporters. Rule number two: Do not talk to strangers. And rule number three—"

Jewel folded her arms and frowned. "You're no fun."

"Exactly. Now, to your room, Missy. No arguments."

Satisfied Jewel was corralled, Charlie Grace straightened her shirt and stepped outside, bracing herself for the reporters circling like buzzards over roadkill.

And lucky her—she was today's special on the menu.

A woman in a too-tight blazer held a microphone aloft. "How does it feel to go from small-town cowgirl to national sensation?"

"No comment," she said.

"No comment," to the second, who demanded to know if she had any idea something this rare was on her property.

"No comment," to all of them as she pushed through, making it clear that no, she would not be answering questions about her financial situation, her overnight success, or what she planned to do with the money.

After what felt like an eternity, the throng seemed to get the hint. She wasn't open to giving them a story. Never mind all the camera flashes that guaranteed her image would be appearing on the evening broadcasts when all she wanted was for nothing to change.

Finally, the news vans packed up and rolled away. Charlie Grace exhaled, squared her shoulders and stepped back inside. She firmly locked the door behind her.

Her sanctuary.

She took a deep breath and leaned against the kitchen counter, trying to take in everything that had happened. Despite her intentions, the *Treasure Pickers* show and their finding had made her life a circus.

Her train of thought was cut short by the television blaring from the living room. And there, in full high-definition betrayal, sat the Knit Wit ladies on a morning talk show, nestled together like they were discussing the best way to bind a quilt —only the topic wasn't quilting. It was her.

"Well, we've known Charlie Grace since she was knee-high to a grasshopper," Dorothy Vaughn declared, adjusting her oversized turquoise necklace. "That girl and her little band of troublemakers—Reva, Lila, Capri—always up to something. Wore the knees out of their jeans climbing trees and chasing boys. And now look at her, all grown up."

Oma Griffith sniffed, leaning in. "We always said she needed a good man to keep her from working herself into an early grave." She smacked Betty Dunning's knee for emphasis. "And wouldn't you know it? Along comes Nick Thatcher, all the way from Hollywood."

"That man," Betty said, fanning herself with the show's cue cards, "has shoulders broad enough to carry her right over the threshold and then some."

"And that jawline," Dorothy added, eyes twinkling. "Like something straight off one of those firefighter calendars."

Cackling. Giggling. One of them actually snorted.

Charlie Grace let out a strangled groan and lunged for the remote, smacking the power button before they started ranking Nick's other assets.

Before she had a moment to react further, her phone buzzed. A text from Reva.

"You'd better get on social media. Gibbs has opened a channel and is monetizing your story...told from an insider."

Charlie Grace dropped her forehead to the counter.

Perfect. Just perfect.

All she ever wanted was a quiet life, a good cup of coffee, and maybe a decent man. Instead, she was one viral post away from needing a disguise at the grocery store.

25

Lila matched her stride to Camille's as they rounded the final stretch of the community center's track. The late morning air had been crisp when they started, but now the sun had crept higher, warming their backs as they slowed to a walk.

"Felt good to get out," Lila said, stretching her arms above her head. "I think spring has sprung."

Camille nodded, but her expression remained distant. She swiped at her forehead with the sleeve of her hoodie, her breathing a little unsteady.

Lila studied her daughter's face. "You okay? You've barely said a word all morning."

Camille hesitated. "Yeah."

Lila wasn't one to hover, but concern prompted her to tilt her head, studying Camille a beat longer. "You sure?"

Camille picked at a loose thread on her sleeve. "Just...tired, I guess."

Lila didn't buy it. Not entirely. But she also knew better than to push too hard. "Didn't sleep last night?"

Camille gave a half-hearted shrug. "Something like that."

The trail behind the community center curved gently past newly budded cottonwoods, their branches stretching toward the sky like waking limbs. Clumps of bright yellow balsamroot swayed beside the path, their petals wide open to the warmth of the midday sun.

Lila slowed her pace, glancing at Camille as they neared the parking lot. "Capri's home now," she said, trying to sound light in tone. She tucked a loose strand of hair behind her ear. "The doctors say she'll heal just fine, but it's been an ordeal. You know Capri—she's probably already plotting how to get back on one of those rafts the second summer rolls around." She shook her head with a small laugh. "Stubborn as ever. Yet, I do think the accident softened her some. She seems…I don't know, quieter in a way. Like she's thinking things through instead of just charging ahead. Of course, knowing Capri, that won't last long."

Lila kicked a stray pebble off the trail, watching it tumble into the grass. "Still, I wouldn't be surprised if she tries to prove she's invincible by the time the first group of tourists shows up with their paddles in hand." She paused.

No response.

Not to be deterred, Lila attempted to engage her daughter again. "Did you hear Jason Griffith is engaged? Oma is beyond thrilled."

Still no response.

A meadowlark darted overhead, its golden breast flashing in the sunlight as it let out a bright, warbling song that drifted across the trail.

"And Charlie Grace—oh, Camille, it's been hullabaloo central with her ever since that picker show found that valuable pocket watch on the ranch. Now the whole town's buzzing about what she's going to do with all that money, and you know how folks love to speculate. Nicola Cavendish is acting like she's Thunder Mountain's personal financial advisor, and Reva

—well, Reva just keeps muttering 'Lord, give me strength' under her breath whenever the subject comes up." She laughed, nudging Camille's shoulder. "It's been wild."

Camille gave a small smile, barely more than a lift of her lips. "Yeah, sounds like a lot," she murmured.

Lila frowned. That wasn't the reaction she expected. Normally, Camille would be laughing, making some sharp-witted comment, but today...something was off. Lila told herself not to read into it. Her baby was pregnant, dealing with all the changes that came with it.

She remembered how it had been for her—how her body had felt like it wasn't her own when she was pregnant with Camille. And how Aaron, sweet and clueless, had tried so hard to keep up. She smiled to herself, thinking of that time at the grocery store when her cravings hit mid-aisle, and she'd suddenly needed a jar of pickles and a pack of Twinkies right that second. Aaron had gone white as a sheet, taking her seriously. He, no doubt, thought she was about to collapse from hunger.

He'd ripped open the Twinkies, stuffing one into her hand like he was delivering life-saving medicine. Then he'd unscrewed the pickle jar with the kind of urgency most men reserved for defusing a bomb. A store clerk had come rushing over, only to find her eight months pregnant and sitting cross-legged on the tile floor, dipping Twinkies into pickle juice while Aaron muttered something about hormones and survival.

She sighed, shaking off the fond memory, and wrapped an arm around Camille's shoulder. "You sure you're okay, baby?"

Camille hesitated, then nodded. "Yeah, Mom. Just tired."

Lila glanced over at Camille, searching her face for something unspoken, but after a moment, she sighed and let it go—for now.

They made their way toward the parking lot, their sneakers crunching over gravel. Lila had come to recognize Camille's silences, the way she retreated into herself when she was wrestling with something. Lila didn't often push—she'd learned long ago that patience got better results than prying.

Still, she couldn't help herself. "You do know you can talk to me about anything, right?"

Camille gave a small nod, but her shoulders remained hunched. They reached the edge of the parking lot, where Lila's SUV was parked among a handful of other vehicles.

Suddenly, Camille stopped. Her body went rigid, her breath catching in her throat.

Lila followed her gaze. Parked near the entrance was a truck, shiny black, its polished chrome grill glinting under the sun.

Camille's fingers curled into fists at her sides. Her breath came quicker, uneven.

Lila grew immediately concerned. "Camille?"

Her daughter's throat bobbed with a hard swallow. "That's his truck."

A chill ran through Lila, cutting through the warmth of the sun. She knew enough to recognize the warning bells blaring in her daughter's demeanor. "Who's truck, Camille?"

Camille kept glancing at the vehicle, her jaw clenched. "I knew this would happen," she murmured. "I knew he'd come looking eventually."

A pang of realization hit Lila, settling deep in her chest. She wrapped an arm around Camille's shoulders, pulling her close. "Baby," she muttered, her voice gentle but firm. "Who's in the truck?"

Camille's hand instinctively went to her belly. "The father."

Lila was confused. "And that's a bad thing?"

She'd wondered about the baby's father for weeks, but every time she'd tried to bring it up, Camille shut down, her answers clipped or nonexistent. Eventually, Lila stopped asking, figuring she'd learn his identity when Camille was ready to spill.

Still, countless questions swirled in Lila's mind.

How had they met? Were they classmates? Where did he live? Did his parents know? And the biggest of all—did Camille love him? Did he love her?

Lila's pulse quickened as she followed her daughter to the waiting truck. She was about to find out.

26

Capri stretched out on the sofa, her injured leg propped up on a pillow. The weight of the cast and the crutches leaning against the coffee table were constant reminders that she wasn't going anywhere anytime soon. She hated it. Being active defined her, and now she was stuck, bored out of her mind.

The television droned on in the background, an endless loop of talking heads, reality shows, and overly dramatic medical dramas. She thumbed the buttons on the remote, flipping through the channels mindlessly.

Channel 7 – A courtroom show where two neighbors screamed at each other over a broken fence. Click.

Channel 14 – A cooking competition where a celebrity chef berated a contestant for overcooked risotto. Click.

Channel 23 – A real estate show in some exotic location where couples argued over which multimillion-dollar mansion to buy. Click.

Channel 47 – A classic Western with a standoff in the middle of a dusty street. Click.

Channel 55 – The local news, leading with another grim headline. Click.

She sighed and turned the television off, tossing the remote onto the cushion beside her. Her head pressed against the back of the sofa, and for a moment, she simply stared at the ceiling.

She reached for her phone. Maybe social media would provide a distraction. She scrolled mindlessly through posts—pictures of friends' kids, vacation snapshots, and a relentless flood of political debates. The comments section was a war zone.

"Ugh," she muttered, locking her phone and dropping it onto her lap. Politics. She was definitely not in the mood for that today.

A thought crossed her mind. She hadn't talked to her mom since leaving the hospital, aside from a few brief texts. The silence gnawed at her. Maybe her mom was just giving her space, but Capri missed hearing her voice, even if their relationship had been strained lately.

She hesitated for a moment, then pulled up her mom's number and pressed the call button. The line rang. Capri tapped her fingers against the armrest, waiting.

"Hello?"

"Hey, Mom." Capri cleared her throat. "Just thought I'd check in."

"Capri, sweetheart. It's so good to hear your voice."

Capri exhaled, a tension she hadn't realized she was carrying loosening just a bit. Maybe this was what she needed —a little normalcy, a little connection.

"So, tell me," her mom said warmly. "How are you?"

Capri launched into a recitation of her current medical condition, taking special note that the doctors were encouraged. "I seem to be healing up nicely."

"Oh, good to hear, sweetheart." There was a pause on the other end of the line. "Honey?"

"Yeah, Mom?"

"I need to cut this short. Earl and I were just about to make a trip to Costco. We go every Tuesday for senior day. Hot dogs for half off." Her mother giggled. "It's our weekly date."

Capri stared at her phone for a long moment, the conversation—or lack of one—still echoing in her ears. A polite but distant *"Gotta go now."* Just a casual dismissal, like they spoke every day instead of weeks slipping by without a word.

"Yeah, okay, Mom." She clicked off the phone without saying goodbye, then set it down on the coffee table. The living room was quiet, save for the steady tick of the clock over the fireplace. A knot formed in her stomach, coiling tighter the more she thought about it.

Her mom had moved on so seamlessly. New husband, new life, a whirlwind of change that left Capri standing on the outside, looking in. Hadn't she given up enough? Held everything together for years while her mother struggled with Dick's addiction? Capri had made sure she was okay, put her own life on hold time and time again. She'd made sure her mom had no financial worries. Even when Dick was sober and going through his cancer treatments, her mother buried her head in the sand, not wanting to face unpleasant things—leaving Capri to deal with the struggle by herself. And now that she'd married again, she barely warranted a five-minute phone call?

She swallowed the lump rising in her throat. She would not —would not—fall apart over this. Never had, never would.

But damn, it hurt.

She grabbed a nearby novel and began skimming the words, flipping the pages with fury. Motion kept emotions in check. At least, that's what she told herself.

But as she tried to read the blurred page, a tear slipped down her cheek anyway.

A sound at the door pulled Capri from her spiraling thoughts. Maybe it was Bodhi. He'd visited nearly every day—

and sometimes twice a day while she was in the hospital and rehab.

She sniffed, wiped the back of her hand across her cheek, and took a steadying breath watching as the door eased open.

"Hey," Jake said, his voice as steady as ever, that quiet, grounding presence she'd come to rely on—though she hated admitting it.

She crossed her arms, pleased. "What are you doing back here already?"

"Brought you some lunch from the Rustic Pine." He held up a bag. "Pete and Annie said to tell you hello."

He moved in her direction, his sharp eyes taking her in like he saw more than she wanted him to. "Had a feeling you could use some company."

Capri rolled her eyes, but it lacked any conviction. "So now you're psychic?"

"Nah." He shrugged. "Just good at reading people. And you, sweetheart, wear your hurt like a neon sign, whether you realize it or not."

Her throat tightened, but she forced out a scoff. "I'm fine. Besides, you only left a few hours ago."

Jake didn't argue. He never did. He just sat down next to her, as if he belonged there, and opened the bag. He took out two wrapped hamburgers and a big container of fries. "Hungry?"

Capri let out a long breath and a mumbled "Thanks" before she took one of the hamburgers. She slowly unwrapped it. "I talked to my mom."

Jake nodded, saying nothing, just giving her space to unravel.

"She brushed me off," Capri admitted, her voice smaller than she liked. "Like I was just another person on her to-do list. We haven't talked in weeks, and she barely even asked how I was doing."

Jake's expression softened, but he didn't do the whole *I'm sorry* thing or try to fix it. Instead, he reached out to tuck a stray piece of hair behind her ear.

"She's missing out," he said simply. "She doesn't even know what she's got in you."

Emotion deep within her gave way. "I know she loves me," she murmured. "It's just—"

"Yeah." Jake didn't need her to explain. He got it.

Without thinking, she leaned into him, resting her forehead against his shoulder. His arms wrapped around her without hesitation, strong and solid, the kind of embrace that said *I'm here* without needing the words.

Jake's arms around her felt safe—more so than anything had in a long time. Something inside Capri cracked wide open, the hurt, the loneliness, the years of holding everything together. It all rushed forward at once, surging into the empty spaces she hadn't even realized were there.

Before she could think, before she could talk herself out of it, she lifted her head from his chest, searching his face. His deep brown eyes were unwavering, watching her, not pushing, not pulling away. Just there.

That was all it took.

She leaned in, pressing her lips to his with a hunger that had nothing to do with passion and everything to do with needing him.

Jake didn't hesitate, didn't make her feel foolish. His hands slid to her back, grounding her as he returned the kiss, slow at first, then deeper. Warmth flooded through her, not heat, but something stronger—something terrifying.

She clung to him, her fingers curling into his shirt, desperate to hold onto this moment, to not feel so alone. Jake responded, his grip tightening, his breath hitching slightly, and for a brief second, she thought—this is it. This is where everything changes.

But then—

Jake pulled back.

Not roughly, not abruptly, but enough. Enough that the loss of him sent a cold rush through her.

Capri blinked up at him, her breath unsteady, her heart hammering. "What...?" The word was barely there, more air than sound.

Jake exhaled slowly, keeping his hands on her shoulders like he was afraid she might bolt.

"Capri," he said, his voice rough but gentle. "Don't get this wrong. I know I said it on the mountain, but—I love you."

His conviction hit her like a freight train, busting through the walls she'd spent years building. She sensed the mood in the room had shifted. She could feel it in the air between them.

"But," he continued, eyes locked onto hers, "I want our first time to be about us. Not about your hurt."

The moment stretched between them, raw and real, and Capri didn't know what to do with it. Her instincts screamed at her to pull away, to fold back into herself, to shove the pain down where he couldn't see it. But Jake wasn't letting her go.

His hands slid down, capturing hers, his hold firm as if he could tether her to the moment, keep her from slipping back into old patterns.

"I'm here," he murmured. "I'm not going anywhere. But I won't let this be a decision you regret later. I want you to be sure."

Capri swallowed hard, her eyes burning. She wanted to argue, to tell him he was wrong, that it wasn't about hurt at all. But deep down, she knew better.

Jake brushed his thumb over her knuckles, waiting, watching, giving her space.

She closed her eyes for a beat, let out a slow breath, and squeezed his hands back. "Okay," she whispered, her voice unsteady.

Jake smiled, just a little, and pulled her into a hug—no rush, no pressure. Just him. Just them.

Capri felt the rush before she could stop it—a surge so powerful it nearly stole her breath. His words echoed in her head. *I'm here. I'm not going anywhere.* And she knew, deep down, that she felt the same. She had for a while. Maybe from the first time he looked at her like she was worth waiting for. Maybe from the moment he bought the stupid porch furniture just so she'd have a welcoming space to come home to.

Her fingers tightened around his, and she swallowed hard, her pulse thundering in her ears. "I'm in this for good, too."

The words slipped out before she could second-guess them, before she could put up the usual walls. But for once, she didn't want to take them back.

Jake went still, like she'd knocked the breath from him. His grip on her hands didn't loosen, but his brows lifted slightly in surprise.

She powered forward before she could lose her nerve. "I've never said that to anyone before and meant it. Never. But I mean it now." She squeezed his hands tighter. "I don't want this to be casual. I don't want to pretend like this is something we can let fade when life gets complicated." Her voice grew stronger, more sure. "I want to choose you, Jake. Every day."

A change shifted in his expression, deep and knowing, like he'd been waiting for this moment, like he'd always known she had it in her.

She exhaled, searching his face, needing to make him understand. "I've spent my whole life trying to control everything—trying to keep people from leaving me. But you..." She shook her head, a shaky laugh escaping. "You're the first person I've ever met who makes me feel safe without me having to hold all the pieces together. You make me feel like I can let go, and I won't fall apart."

Jake's lips parted, his eyes now raw and unreadable. But before he could say anything—before she could overthink this—she blurted, "Marry me."

Silence.

Capri barely heard the sound of her own breath over the roaring in her ears. It wasn't planned. It wasn't calculated. It was just true.

Jake blinked, clearly caught off guard. "What?"

She let out a nervous laugh, suddenly aware that her heart was slamming against her ribs. "You heard me."

His lips parted slightly, then pressed together as if he were trying to process what had just happened.

Capri's stomach clenched. Maybe she'd said too much. Maybe she'd ruined everything. But she meant it. She didn't want to go another day pretending she didn't know exactly what she wanted.

And what she wanted was him.

"You and me, huh?" she murmured, her voice unsteady. "What do you say?"

Jake pulled back just enough to better look at her, his eyes shining with something so sure, so unshakable, it took her breath away.

"You and me, Capri," he said, voice low and full of promise. "Always."

She closed her eyes for a beat, letting the moment sink in before letting out a chuckle of pure delight. "Hear that? My heart is pounding."

Jake squeezed her hand and pressed it to his chest. "My heart is pounding too, just so you know."

She couldn't stop the tears.

At last, the future wasn't a source of fear—it was a promise to reach for. She no longer shouldered the weight of going it alone, of always being the one to hold everything together.

She wasn't just looking ahead—she was charging toward a life she wanted, a future full of possibility. The days ahead weren't uncertain; they were wide open, waiting to be filled with love, adventure, and a life she was ready to embrace.

She was exactly where she was meant to be, beside the man she chose—the man who chose her right back.

27

The guy eased out of the driver's side door and leaned against the side of his glossy black pickup, the kind of truck that never saw a dirt road, let alone a hard day's work. His arms were crossed over his chest, and one boot was propped against the tire, the perfect picture of ease, like he had all the time in the world.

Sunlight caught the expensive watch peeking from beneath the cuff of his tailored jacket—a brand most kids his age wouldn't even recognize, let alone afford. His blond hair was expertly tousled, just enough to look effortless, and his smirk deepened as he watched them approach.

"Well, well," he drawled, pushing off the truck with a lazy grace. "I was starting to think you were avoiding me, Camille." His eyes flicked briefly to Lila, full of casual assessment, then back to Camille, as if her mother didn't exist. "That's no way to treat a guy who's got a vested interest, now is it?"

Camille crossed her arms, glaring. "How'd you find me?"

"Wasn't hard. All it took was a couple of casual questions, and this town was more than willing to serve up the answers."

A tense beat passed before Camille huffed, clearly unimpressed. Shifting gears, she gestured between them. "Mom, this is Blaine Newcomb." She turned back to him, her tone flat. "This is my mom."

"Well, hello Camille's mom." He extended a hand. "I'm Senator Newcomb's son."

His tone was smooth, just shy of condescending, the kind of confidence that came from knowing his last name carried weight—at least in some circles in this state.

"Speaking of moms, mine is sitting at a bar and grill in town. She wants to talk with you, Camille."

Was he...smirking?

Lila barely hid her scowl. "That would be the Rustic Pine. Pete and Annie Cumberland are the owners. Friends of ours." She wasn't sure why she was rambling.

Blaine shrugged, like none of this was particularly important to him, but the way he watched Camille told a different story. "Yeah, Rustic Pine. That's the one." His gaze lingered on her, his smirk fading into a look of expectation. "She's waiting for you."

Camille shifted beside Lila, her shoulders tense. "I...I don't know if now is a good time."

Blaine sighed through his nose, like he was already tired of this conversation. "Cami, come on. She just wants to talk. You can't keep hiding from this...situation." His voice was smooth, even, but beneath the polished exterior was an unmistakable edge as his gaze dropped to her slightly swollen belly.

Lila's gaze darted to her daughter, catching the flicker of hesitation in her expression and something else—reluctance, maybe even shame.

Lila's stomach tightened. Understanding was now dawning.

Blaine opened the truck door like it was the most natural thing in the world. "Let's go. We'll take my truck."

Camille didn't move. "I'll ride with my mom."

Blaine grabbed her arm, then immediately released it.

For the briefest second, something dark flashed in Blaine's eyes, but he masked it quickly, his smirk sliding back into place. "Suit yourself," he said, stepping back. But the way he watched Camille, as if waiting for her to change her mind, made Lila's unease settle deeper.

Camille turned away first, walking toward Lila's SUV with deliberate steps. Lila followed, her pulse ticking a little faster than before.

She didn't know the full story yet, but one thing was certain—Camille and this boy might have created a life together, but there was no warmth between them. Lila recognized his type instantly—entitled, self-assured, the kind of young man who expected the world, and the people in it, to fall in line.

He clearly thought her daughter would be no different.

But he was wrong.

Lila had spent years raising Camille to stand strong, and she sure as heavens wasn't going to let some cocky rich kid try to steer her now.

28

Lila pushed open the heavy wooden door of the Rustic Pine, expecting the usual low hum of conversation and the clinking of beer glasses, but instead, silence greeted her. The bar, usually packed with locals, was nearly empty. The faint strains of a country song drifted from the jukebox, and the warm glow of the antler chandeliers cast long shadows across the polished wooden floor.

The scent of grilled meat and fried onions still lingered in the air, mingling with the faint smokiness from the massive stone fireplace in the corner. A few empty glasses sat abandoned on tables, remnants of a lunch crowd that had long since cleared out. The only other sign of life in the place, besides Pete and Annie behind the bar, was Chet Olson, the town's ever-reliable Amazon delivery man, who was hunched over a plate at the bar, cutting into a chicken-fried steak with singular focus.

Chet was a lanky man with a weathered face, a permanent cap of salt-and-pepper stubble, and a habit of talking to himself when he thought no one was listening. His faded blue uniform shirt was unbuttoned at the collar, the sleeves rolled up to his elbows, as if he'd come straight from a long shift. He took a slow bite, chewed thoughtfully, then nodded to himself as if mentally rating the meal.

Annie, drying a glass with a dish towel, arched an eyebrow at him. "Good as always, Chet?"

Chet swallowed, then stabbed another piece with his fork. "Ain't never had a bad one, Annie." He took a sip of iced tea and glanced over as Lila and Camille walked in. "Ladies."

Pastor Pete wiped his hands on a rag and grinned. "You've got the place to yourselves tonight. Everyone cleared out early."

Lila nodded, her gaze sweeping the room before landing on a single occupied table in the farthest corner.

Blaine Newcomb and his mother—better known as the interminable Senator Claudia Newcomb, whose air of disapproval was so thick you could slice it with a steak knife.

She sat ramrod straight at a small table, her spine as unyielding as the high-backed chair she occupied. Everything about her screamed out of place—from her perfectly tailored cream-colored jacket and cashmere sweater to the way she held a martini glass between her delicate fingers, as if reluctant to let it touch her skin.

Her short, icy blonde hair was styled with precision, not a strand out of place, and her jewelry—nothing oversized or gaudy, just expensive—gleamed in the dim lighting. The expression on her face was impossible to miss—lips pressed into a thin, unamused line, nose slightly wrinkled, eyes scanning the room with the air of someone who had just stepped into a particularly distasteful situation.

Lila slowed her steps.

Claudia's sharp gaze flicked toward them before settling on Lila. There was no warmth in her expression, no polite nod of acknowledgment—just a cool, assessing look, as if she were deciding whether to acknowledge their presence at all.

Lila swallowed the urge to react in some way. Instead, she

lifted her chin and slid into an empty chair before introducing herself. "Hello, I'm Lila Bellamy. Camille's mother."

The woman stared back. "Claudia Newcomb—*Senator* Claudia Newcomb." She turned to Camille. "You must be Camille."

Camille nodded. "Nice to meet you."

Blaine raised an arm and snapped his fingers, a sharp, impatient sound that cut through the low hum of conversation. Pete, standing behind the bar, caught the motion and hustled over, wiping his hands on a bar towel.

"What can I get you?" Pete asked, keeping his tone neutral despite the rude summons.

"Double cheeseburger—Swiss, no cheddar. And sweet pickles. No dill," Blaine ordered, his voice leaving no room for negotiation.

Without a glance towards her, Blaine ordered for Camille. "She'll have a salad with ranch on the side and a to-go container," he said, then leaned back, smirking. "Just because you're pregnant doesn't mean you want to get fat."

Lila stilled. The casual cruelty in his voice made her stomach turn. She opened her mouth to respond, then thought better of it. It was unmistakable. This situation radiated risk. She didn't want to add to her daughter's predicament—a dilemma that was clarifying by the moment.

Camille's face burned red, but she didn't immediately respond. Across from her, Claudia lifted her martini glass to her lips, eyes glittering with approval.

Pete hesitated, his hand tightening around the order pad. His gaze flicked to Camille, waiting to see if she'd correct Blaine.

And Lord help her, despite her promise, Lila was about two seconds away from doing it for her.

Camille inhaled sharply, then straightened. "I'll actually

have a grilled chicken sandwich," she said, voice steady. "And fries."

Blaine's jaw ticked. "Camille."

"What?" She folded her arms, her chin lifting just slightly, just enough for Lila to see the spark of defiance underneath the careful control.

Blaine exhaled slowly, shaking his head as if she'd disappointed him. "Fine. But don't complain later when your jeans don't fit."

Claudia chuckled softly, like this was all so amusing.

Pete jotted the order down and walked off without waiting for another word. Knowing Pastor Pete like she did, he was likely sending up a much-needed prayer.

Lila felt heat build under her collar, a familiar anger pressing in. She'd seen this before—the way some men disguised control as care, wrapped it in neat little packages of "concern" and "looking out for you."

It wasn't care. It was power.

Camille sat perfectly still for a long moment, her fingers white-knuckling the edge of the table. Then, slowly, she reached for her water, took a careful sip, and met Blaine's gaze with a steadiness that made Lila's chest tighten.

"You know what, Blaine?" Camille set the glass down, her voice quiet but unwavering. "You don't have to worry about what I eat ever again."

Blaine frowned. "What's that supposed to mean?"

Camille reached for her purse, pushed back her chair, and stood. "It means I'm done."

Lila's breath caught.

Blaine blinked, as if the words didn't register. "Camille—?"

But she was already walking, her back straight, her steps sure, heading for the door with more confidence than Lila had ever seen her carry before.

For a second, the whole bar seemed to hold its breath.

Then Lila exhaled, a slow smile creeping up the corners of her mouth.

Atta girl.

Claudia lifted her martini glass, took a measured sip, and turned away as if the entire room no longer held anything of interest.

Lila had had enough. She stood and let her napkin fall to the table.

"I suggest you sit down," Claudia told her.

"I beg your pardon?"

Claudia reached in her Louis Vuitton bag and retrieved a sealed envelope. She slid it across the table in Lila's direction. "Inside is the name and contact information for my attorney. He's drawn up relinquishment papers, which Blaine will sign." She gave a pointed look. "Provided your daughter signs the NDA clause—and agrees to the nondisclosure of my son as father. She will not put Blaine's name on the birth certificate and will maintain complete discretion, not revealing his name or claiming paternity. There is also a check in a generous amount." Then, she added, "In case Camille still wants to change her mind."

Lila gasped. "She's nearly five months along."

Claudia shrugged before lowering her voice. "These things can be safely arranged."

Lila shook her head vehemently. "No. She's already made her decision."

"Fine. In that event, a bank account has been established. Monthly deposits will be made. Everything is outlined in the relinquishment papers. And I've discreetly arranged for court approval of my son's termination of rights."

Lila turned to Blaine. "Are you okay with this?"

Blaine leaned back, stretching his legs out like the conversation bored him. He shrugged and looked toward Pete at the bar, tapping a finger against his empty glass.

"Look, it's not like I didn't think it through." His tone easy, almost dismissive. "The kid has a mother, and Camille will handle it. I mean, you did. Best thing I can do is step back and let her. No need to drag everyone through unnecessary drama."

Claudia clasped her perfectly manicured hands together, her expression calm, unwavering. She didn't so much as glance at Lila, her focus entirely on Blaine.

"That's right, sweetheart. You have your whole life ahead of you. One misstep doesn't define a man—don't let it. You've worked too hard, and you have too much potential to be tied down by a fleeting one-night stand that was never meant to be permanent." She tilted her head slightly, gave him that knowing look. "The girl will manage. Women always do. But you? You have a future—one too bright to let a single mistake dim your potential."

She finally glanced at Lila, smooth and unreadable, before returning her gaze to Blaine. "You're making the right choice."

Pete arrived with the plate, setting it down in front of Blaine with a slight thud. The burger rested under the dim lighting, unmistakable yellow cheddar oozing over the edges of the grilled meat.

Lila caught Pete's eye, and he gave her the barest flicker of amusement before nodding toward the ketchup bottle. No words, just a silent acknowledgment. Then, without waiting for a reaction, he wiped his hands on his bar towel and slipped away.

Blaine picked up the burger, completely unaware.

Lila folded her arms against her chest and fixed them both with a steady gaze. "This is Camille's decision," she said firmly, feeling the blood pump through her neck veins.

Claudia pressed the sealed envelope closer, her expression stoic. "Take it. I'm sure she'll agree." She paused, then added, "Besides, I understand she is intent on a career in film. She wouldn't want anything to mar her chances of breaking into the industry, even given Nick Thatcher's help."

The barely disguised threat slithered between them, but Lila heard it loud and clear. Disgust churned in her stomach.

These people. Cold. Calculating. So convinced they could manipulate Camille's future with a few carefully chosen words and a check.

It was hard to look at the truth when it ran contrary to what she wanted to believe. But the thought of them near her future grandbaby made her skin crawl.

Without further hesitation, Lila took the envelope and tucked it into her back pocket. Then, leveling Claudia with a razor-sharp look, she let a slow smile curve her lips.

"You know, *Senator*, for someone who's likely spent a lifetime buying influence, you sure don't know much about real power."

And with that, Lila spun and walked away, leaving them both to sit in their own entitlement.

29

A spring breeze stirred the evening air, carrying the scent of damp earth and the promise of new beginnings. Capri sat on the porch of her cabin, bathed in the soft glow of the string lights draped along the beams. The bulbs swayed gently, casting golden halos against the night. Overhead, a full moon hung in the sky, luminous and whole, watching over Thunder Mountain with quiet wisdom.

Capri adjusted her position in the rocking chair, her crutches resting against the railing beside her. The ache in her leg was a dull reminder of all she had been through, but she felt lighter tonight.

Lila, Reva, and Charlie Grace bustled around, bringing out more snacks, uncorking a bottle of wine, and arranging themselves comfortably on the cushioned seats of Capri's new patio furniture—the set Jake had picked out for her.

"Man's got good taste," Reva admitted, patting one of the chairs as she sat down.

The front door creaked open, and Jake stepped out. He was freshly showered, his dark hair still damp at the edges. Without a word, he walked over to Capri, brushing a loose strand of hair behind her ear before pressing a kiss to the top of her head. "I'll be home later," he murmured, his voice warm and steady.

She tilted her face up to him, her heart skipping in a way she still hadn't gotten used to. "Don't be too late."

The girlfriends chuckled, and Capri rolled her eyes. "What?"

Charlie Grace filled the wine glasses. "Nothing. You just seem...I don't know."

"Like an old married couple," Lila finished.

Capri and Jake exchanged amused glances before he turned to go. With a lingering glance, he stepped off the porch and into the night, his silhouette disappearing down the gravel drive.

The moonlight caught on the trees, casting silver-edged shadows across the yard as she heard him start the engine and pull away.

Charlie Grace sighed dreamily. "That man is smitten."

Capri waved off the comment. "He's...well, he's Jake. That's saying a lot."

Charlie Grace handed her a glass of wine. "Oh, it's saying plenty."

Capri worked to keep her face neutral. "It's saying he's Jake. That's all." She wouldn't be able to keep the secret for much longer, but for now, it was hers—untouched by opinions, unshaken by questions, a quiet joy she could hold close just a little while longer.

Lila exchanged a knowing glance with Reva. "That's all?"

Reva tilted her head, studying Capri like a puzzle missing its last piece. "Funny. I seem to remember a time when you barely tolerated the guy."

Capri shrugged, keeping her voice light. "People evolve."

Charlie Grace folded her arms. "Uh-huh. And what exactly has Jake evolved into?"

Capri busied herself by swirling the wine in her glass, watching as the legs ran down the sides. "He's...dependable."

Charlie Grace let out a dry laugh. "So is my dog."

Capri shot her a look. "Fine. He's kind. Thoughtful. He listens." She stopped, realizing she was saying too much. "And he's handy with a hammer."

Lila narrowed her eyes. "I don't know, Capri. You sound suspiciously like a woman in love."

Capri forced a laugh, reaching for a deviled egg off the platter. "So, what if I am?"

Reva pressed a hand to her chest, eyes twinkling. "So, you admit you have feelings for Jake?"

Capri fumbled the deviled egg, nearly sending it rolling off her plate. She recovered fast, popping it into her mouth and chewing, buying herself a second to steady her pulse. "Let's talk about something else," she mumbled around the bite, avoiding their knowing stares.

Later. She'd tell them later. But for now, she just smiled and changed the subject. "So, Charlie Grace, what's new with you? I know you've been busy since the big find. Give us a full update."

Charlie Grace leaned back in her chair, stretching her arms overhead with a satisfied sigh. "So, it's done. The trusts are officially in place for Dad and Jewel—airtight. Gibbs can huff and puff all he wants, but he won't weasel a dime."

Reva gave an approving nod. "Smart move. That man could charm a snake out of its skin, but even a snake knows better than to steal what it can't swallow."

Charlie Grace smiled, but it didn't quite reach her eyes. "That was priority one. The second? I set up a foundation and fully funded it for Thunder Mountain. The town's been good to me, and I wanted to give back. The money will go toward community projects, emergency relief, scholarships. I've named it after Alf Morgan, the original owner of the trunk—and I've appointed the three of you as the trustees. Providing you agree to serve."

Lila's eyes widened. "Charlie Grace, that's incredible."

Capri let out a low whistle. "That's a legacy move."

Reva's eyes lit up. "And what an honor it is. Of course, we'll serve—right, girls?"

Charlie Grace grinned, their reactions seeming to fill her with warmth. "I just want to make sure this place thrives for years to come. Which brings me to the next big thing—expanding Teton Trails Guest Ranch."

She leaned forward, excitement flickering in her gaze. "I've already hired contractors. We're adding new luxury cabins—still rustic but with high-end amenities. Think stone fireplaces, deep soaking tubs, heated floors. The kind of place where you can spend the day riding trails and come back to something first-class."

Reva grinned. "That's smart. People want the charm of the mountains but the comfort of a resort."

"Exactly," Charlie Grace said. "We're also expanding the main lodge—bigger dining space, a full-service spa, and a yoga deck overlooking the valley. I've even brought in a marketing company to help put us on the map. High-end travel magazines, influencers, custom branding—the whole deal."

Lila shook her head, impressed. "You're turning this place into a world-class destination."

"That's the goal," Charlie Grace admitted. Then she grew quiet, her gaze drifting out toward the spread of pines beyond the porch. "You know, I was thinking earlier...remember when you girls built the first website for the ranch? How you helped me get this place off the ground?"

Capri smiled. "How could we forget? You were starting your guest ranch on a wing and a prayer. It was the least we could do to help."

Lila shook her head with a soft smile. "That's what friends do. This town has a way of showing up for each other, and that's what makes Thunder Mountain so special—the kind of place I want my grandbaby to grow up in."

Capri topped off her glass. "How's Camille holding up? Is the morning sickness finally letting up?"

Lila let out a sharp breath, her fingers tightening around her glass. "Yes, she's doing better. And I finally met the father—Blaine Newcomb. Had the pleasure of a little sit-down with him and his mother at the Rustic Pine...Senator Newcomb, in case you didn't make the connection."

Charlie Grace arched an eyebrow. "That doesn't sound good. And judging by the look on your face, it wasn't. What happened?"

Reva set down her fork, sensing trouble. "Yes, what did they want?"

Lila let out a humorless laugh, still shaking her head at the sheer audacity of it. "We walked into a business negotiation that felt like a trap." She took a sip of her drink before continuing. "Claudia Newcomb did most of the talking. Said they've been 'considering all options' and decided it would be best for everyone—especially Camille—if Blaine legally relinquished his rights to the baby."

Silence fell over the table as her friends absorbed the weight of those words.

Capri frowned. "Wait. He wants to sign away his rights? Just like that?"

Lila gave a slow nod, her expression filled with disgust. "And all Camille had to do was sign an NDA, ensuring Camille and the baby never so much as whisper the Newcomb name again. Especially in public."

Charlie Grace leaned back, arms crossed against her chest. "Unbelievable. That coward's skipping out, and his mother's sweeping his mess under the rug?"

"Oh, she spun it beautifully," Lila said with a dry laugh. "Said it would 'free Camille' from any unnecessary complications, allow her to start fresh without the burden of messy entanglements." Her fingers tightened around her glass. "As if that baby is an inconvenience instead of a human being. As if Camille hasn't spent months agonizing over how to do what's best."

Reva's jaw clenched. "What did you say?"

Lila met her gaze, fire sparking in her eyes. "I told them that Camille would decide what's best for her child."

Capri exhaled, shaking her head. "And what did they say to that?"

Lila gave a humorless smile. "The senator gave me that patronizing little smirk of hers and said...and I'm summarizing. But I was 'letting emotions cloud my judgment.' That it was a 'generous offer' and I should 'encourage Camille to be pragmatic.'" Her voice dripped with sarcasm. "Oh, and of course, they'd ensure 'discreet financial assistance.' You know, to soften the blow."

Reva scoffed. "So, they want to throw money at her, erase the whole thing, and waltz back into their perfect little world?" She shook her head, letting out a dry laugh. "If secrecy was their top priority, maybe they shouldn't have chosen the Rustic Pine for their big cover-up meeting. Do they even know how small towns work? Keeping secrets isn't exactly our strong suit."

"Exactly." Lila set her glass down, shaking her head. "And Blaine just sat there the whole time, nodding along, barely looking me in the eye. Like a spineless little puppet."

Charlie Grace huffed. "Please tell me you told them where to shove their NDA."

Lila's smirk returned, this time edged with steel. "Oh, I did. I told them Camille has more backbone in her pinky than Blaine ever will—and that this family doesn't take hush money." She hesitated for a beat, then added, "But honestly? Blaine Newcomb is controlling, and the thought of him having any influence over Camille and the baby unsettles me. Maybe this isn't just them cutting ties. Maybe it's God protecting my daughter."

Capri nodded her approval. "Darn right."

Reva exhaled, shaking her head in disbelief. "What now?"

Lila's expression softened. "That's up to Camille. But whatever she decides, she's not alone in this. And she sure doesn't need nasty people like them dictating her future."

Her friends nodded, a silent agreement passing between them. No matter what happened next, they would stand by Camille—and Lila—every step of the way.

Then, as if sensing the heavy turn of the conversation, Charlie Grace exhaled and leaned forward, a mischievous glint in her eye. "Well, if we're talking about things getting out of hand, can we discuss the spectacle that Jason Griffith's wedding is turning into?"

Reva groaned, rubbing her temples. "Oh, don't get me started. His mother, Oma, and the Knit Wits have officially lost their minds."

Capri leaned in with a smirk forming. "All right, hit me with the latest."

Charlie Grace exhaled. "Oh, you have no idea. His mother and the Knit Wits have taken over, and now the whole thing is turning into some kind of over-the-top spectacle."

Reva nodded. "Apparently, they think the Bluebird Bookstore is such a pillar of Jason's identity that they want to incorporate it into the wedding theme. They've decided every guest should receive a custom leather-bound book as a favor."

Lila raised an eyebrow. "Who's funding this? The Library of Congress?"

Charlie Grace shook her head. "And that's just the start. Oma's convinced that because Jason loves birdwatching, they need actual bluebirds in decorative cages at the reception—for ambiance."

Capri broke into laughter. "Oh, sure. Nothing says romance

like a bunch of panicked birds flapping around in the middle of dinner."

Reva leaned in. "And get this—since Jason's a mystery lover, they're seriously considering turning the rehearsal dinner into a full-blown Agatha Christie-style murder mystery dinner. With actors. Costumes. Clues hidden under the dinner plates."

Lila pinched the bridge of her nose. "So instead of a quiet celebration, it's going to be an elaborate whodunit with a bunch of guests trying to figure out who 'poisoned' the groom?"

Charlie Grace sighed. "At this point, I half expect Jason's fiancée to call the whole thing off and elope in the mountains just to get away from it."

"Oh, it gets better," Reva added, crossing her arms. "Oma wants the flower girls to release actual doves at the end of the ceremony. She says it'll be symbolic of her boy's love taking flight."

Charlie Grace slipped off her boots and tucked her feet beneath her. "Then you have the Knit Wits, who've taken it upon themselves to handcraft individual quilted seat covers for every guest, in case the chairs at the reception aren't comfortable enough."

Capri's mouth fell open. "Please tell me you're joking."

Reva sighed. "Oh, I wish. But no, they're stitching away like it's the Olympics of needlework. Each one has Jason and his fiancée's initials and a personalized quote about love."

Charlie Grace swirled the deep red liquid in her glass, not bothering to mask her amusement. "I hear Gibbs' says, 'True love waits...but he never could.'"

Capri laughed. "Okay, that's kind of perfect. Especially given his track record with women."

Reva tilted her head and groaned. "I'm starting to think the biggest challenge of this wedding won't be saying 'I do'—it'll be surviving the planning process."

Capri dabbed a napkin at the corner of her mouth. "Well,

one thing's for sure...their wedding is going to be unforgettable."

She hesitated for half a beat, then drew in a breath, her fingers smoothing the napkin against the table. "Speaking of weddings...I guess it's time I told you all—I'm getting married."

The words landed like a stone in a still pond, sending ripples of stunned silence across the table.

Charlie Grace blinked. "Wait. What?"

Reva sat up straighter. "Capri Jacobs, did you just drop that like it was nothing?"

Lila's eyes widened. "To Jake?"

Capri let out a slow breath, a small, private smile tugging at her lips. "Yes. To Jake." She met their gazes, bracing for the inevitable onslaught of reactions. "It just feels right. So...we're doing it."

The stunned silence held for a fraction longer before all three women erupted at once—talking over each other, demanding details, peppering her with questions.

Capri leaned back, letting them have their moment. She had always been the restless one, the wild heart who chased adventure and outran anything that felt too permanent. Commitment had never been her language, and love—the real kind, the kind that stayed—had always felt like something meant for other people.

But this? This was different. Her decision to marry Jake was the one choice she was certain of.

Capri let the moment settle over her. The love, the friendship, the unwavering sense of home.

Her gaze drifted upward to the moon spilling its soft light over the world. It had always been there, watching, waiting. And for the first time, she wasn't running, wasn't hiding in the shadows.

She was learning to stand in its glow.

AUTHOR'S NOTE

Hello, Readers!

A heartfelt thank you for reading the Teton Mountain Series. These books celebrate the invaluable role of friendships. I am thankful to have girlfriends I've known since high school. These women bless me beyond what I can describe.

The spark for these stories was my own experiences of profound friendship, a theme I've always wanted to explore in my writing.

A trip to Yellowstone National Park and the Teton Mountain National Park in Wyoming inspired the setting. For any of you who have followed me, you know I thrill to take my readers to places I love to vacation. In these books, you'll be whisked away to the majestic Teton Mountains, you'll dine in the trendy restaurants in Jackson Hole, and see bears and moose in secluded pinewood forests. You'll experience herds of buffalo roaming the meadows of Hayden Valley and hike the backcountry trails around crystal blue lakes lined with pastel-colored lupine blooms. The town of Thunder Mountain is a fictionalized community based upon DuBois, Wyoming—a charming western town with wooden boardwalks and quaint buildings lining its Main Street. I took a little liberty as an author and relocated it to where Moran is now on the map.

Mostly, I created four women friends who have become so very dear to me as I've placed them on the pages of these books—Charlie Grace, Reva, Lila and Capri.

I hope you enjoy the time spent with us!

Kellie Coates Gilbert

ABOUT THE AUTHOR

USA Today Bestselling Author Kellie Coates Gilbert has won readers' hearts with her heartwarming and highly emotional stories about women and the relationships that define their lives. As a former legal investigator, Kellie brings a unique blend of insight and authenticity to her stories, ensuring that readers are hooked from the very first page.

In addition to garnering hundreds of five-star reviews, Kellie has been described by RT Book Reviews as a "deft, crisp storyteller." Her books were featured as Barnes & Noble Top

Shelf Picks and earned a coveted place on Library Journal's Best Book List.

Born and raised amidst the breathtaking beauty of Sun Valley, Idaho, Kellie draws inspiration from the vibrant landscapes of her youth, infusing her stories with a vivid sense of place. Kellie now lives with her husband of over thirty-five years in Dallas, where she spends most days by her pool drinking sweet tea and writing the stories of her heart.

Learn more about Kellie and her books at www.kelliecoatesgilbert.com

Enjoy special discounts by buying direct from Kellie at www.kelliecoatesgilbertbooks.com

ALSO BY KELLIE COATES GILBERT

Dear Readers,

Thank you for reading this story. If you'd like to read more of my books, please check out these series. To purchase at special discounts: www.kelliecoatesgilbertbooks.com

TETON MOUNTAIN SERIES

Where We Belong – Book 1

Echoes of the Heart – Book 2

Holding the Dream – Book 3

As the Sun Rises – Book 4

Losing the Moon – Book 5

Friends are Forever – Book 6

A Teton Mountain Christmas – Book 7

MAUI ISLAND SERIES

Under the Maui Sky – Book 1

Silver Island Moon – Book 2

Tides of Paradise – Book 3

The Last Aloha – Book 4

Ohana Sunrise – Book 5

Sweet Plumeria Dawn – Book 6

Songs of the Rainbow – Book 7

Hibiscus Christmas – Book 8

PACIFIC BAY SERIES

Chances Are – Book 1

Remember Us – Book 2

Chasing Wind – Book 3

Between Rains – Book 4

SUN VALLEY SERIES

Sisters – Book 1

Heartbeats – Book 2

Changes – Book 3

Promises – Book 4

TEXAS GOLD COLLECTION

A Woman of Fortune – Book 1

Where Rivers Part – Book 2

A Reason to Stay – Book 3

What Matters Most – Book 4

STAND ALONE NOVELS:

Mother of Pearl

AVAILABLE AT ALL MAJOR RETAILERS

FOR EXCLUSIVE DISCOUNTS:

www.kelliecoatesgilbertbooks.com

Made in the USA
Monee, IL
03 August 2025